IDOL BONES

IDOL BONES

D. M. Greenwood

Chivers Press
Bath, Avon, England

Thorndike Press
Thorndike, Maine USA

This Large Print edition is published by Chivers Press, England and by Thorndike Press, USA.

Published in 1995 in the U.K. by arrangement with Headline Publishing Limited.

Published in 1995 in the U.S. by arrangement with St. Martin's Press, Inc.

U.K. Hardcover ISBN 0–7451–3056–9 (Chivers Large Print)
U.K. Softcover ISBN 0–7451–3068–2 (Camden Large Print)
U.S. Softcover ISBN 0–7862–0401–X (General Series Edition)

The text of this Large Print edition is unabridged.
Other aspects of the book may vary from the original edition.

Set in 16 pt. New Times Roman.

Printed in Great Britain on acid-free paper.

British Library Cataloguing in Publication Data available

Library of Congress Cataloging-in-Publication Data

Greenwood, D. M. (Diane M.)
Idol bones / D. M. Greenwood.
p. cm.
ISBN 0–7862–0401–X (lg. print : lsc)
1. Large type books. I. Title.
PR6057.R376I36 1995
823′.914—dc20 94–44653

To
Philip Tyrrell

CONTENTS

CHAPTER ONE

A VIEW FROM A PEW

The article in the *Bow Examiner* was on the centre page between 'Local Firm's Success in World Seed Drill Market' and 'City Striker's Sci-Fi Goal'. It was headed 'A View from a Pew'.

'Have you ever seen a new dean put into his cathedral? If you haven't, you wouldn't learn too much about it from the order of service sheet for the induction of Dean Vincent Stream this Sunday at Bow St Aelfric. It has three hymns printed on it, mentions three processions and concludes with some threatening remarks against rushing the exits before the last of the processions has left.

'So the fanfare took us all by surprise. Bow St Aelfric's Youth Orchestra silver section weren't quite together to start with, but they got better or at least louder as they went on. When they'd finished there was a longish pause. Surely they couldn't have lost a hundred clergy? Bow St Aelfric is one of England's smaller cathedrals, and a hundred clergy, many of them in cassock albs, queuing at the wrong door would be noticeable.

'To keep us alert, there was a rustle of people preparing to stand up and then deciding not to.

The order of service was no help. An enormous canon dressed like a wizard, in gold cope with modern Picassoesque embroidery on the back, ambled very slowly down the nave aisle. A tiny messenger boy of about twelve raced after him. The boy, dressed in new era postman's blue with very broad red stripes down the side of his trousers, wore spurs which seemed unfamiliar to him. The boy's friends recognised him as the chairman of the chemical manufacturers, CBL, dressed as the Lord Lieutenant of the county for the afternoon. The enormous canon took him by the scruff of the neck and stowed him at the end of a pew of mayors and mayoresses. He looked relieved to have found a safe slot and allowed his knees to sag, possibly supposing that he was praying.

'By this point the audience (you couldn't call us a congregation) had been waiting thirty-five minutes. The organ had finished playing fifteen minutes previously with a finality suggesting the organist had locked up the instrument and gone away on holiday. So the first procession slid in and got halfway down the nave before anyone noticed. We stumbled to our feet once more. The choir, four barrel-chested men, twelve young, pretty diminutive women and a dégagé ("we've been here before—often") rout of choirboys, failed to co-ordinate its steps. Some waltzed, some czadased, others tangoed, to avoid treading on the too frequent feet of those in front or behind them. There's something eerie about a procession processing to no music. There's nothing to cover up mistakes.

'The second procession, made up of clergy, was luckier. The reserve organist had been wrenched from the bosom of his family (Sunday afternoon) and eased into place. He caught up with them, before they reached the crossing. Thought had gone into this procession. Long had been paired with short, thin with fat, old with young. Thus did they exemplify the diversity of creation. Many of them had an air of having been awakened from deep sleep, many were limping; arthritis is an occupational hazard for the clergy—all that suppressed anger. The nave altar steps were greeted with enormous surprise. "What have we here? Never seen these before have you, Dick?" But up they sprang. Many of them made the top step and those who didn't were Christianly helped up by their brothers. At their rear came six female deacons in blue suits with arranged expressions. They marched like military policemen, in step, making their point. They carried handbags to show they were women and wore dog collars to indicate the other thing.

'The final procession represented other denominations and faiths. Some thoughtful pairing for maximum effect had gone on here too. The purple soutane and silver hair (matching the silvery white crocheting on his cotta) of the RC Monsignor contrasted well with the austere black suit and dapper bonnet of the Salvation Army lady. The Methodist in academicals (Sheffield MSc by the look of it) had been paired with the rabbi who did not take off his hat. The URC man in a dark lounge suit got a verger, owing to being accompanied by a black bishop, who looked as though he might know how to guard his flock, even with a kalashnikov, if necessary, in the cause of a just war.

'The diocesan bishop distanced himself from this rout by some ten paces and showed he was at home on his own patch by smiling at both sides of the audience. Dean Stream, we were led to believe, would come on a bit later when he knocked to be allowed in at the already open west door.

'Then things speeded up a lot. We sang a swift hymn (organist eager to return to family?), heard a reading from the remoter regions of the Old Testament in the New English Bible version which, even had the audio system been working, would not have been too meaningful. The Lord Lieutenant disconnected his spurs from each other and read the letters patent. It became clear that this was the point of the entire show. Nothing about God but a fair amount about the Queen. The bishop sat on a papier mâché throne on loan from the Bow St Aelfric Light Opera company, surrounded by five men in court gowns and wigs who clearly knew exactly what the letters patent meant. The message was plain. It was a legal charade. It was about temporal, worldly power. It had nothing to do with worship or the spirit.

'The new dean decided to start as he meant to go on. He evaded his own verger, mounted the pulpit before the precentor could read a second lesson and embarked on his sermon. The precentor's verger looked daggers at the dean's verger and steered the thwarted precentor back to his stall with the air of having to replace the stopper in the decanter before a drop could be poured. The new dean preached about Solzhenitsyn under the impression that he represented the best modern Christian thought. The precentor plotted revenge. The final hymn saw the three processions move off at twice the speed of light and the audience reached for its car keys.

'There was a time when the Anglican church knew its way about in matters of ceremonial. The clergy knew what cathedrals were for. Now they feel they've got to write their own scenarios to show their own values, and, indeed, they do convey those values only too well. But if you thought this rigmarole had anything to do with celebrating spiritual life, if you thought it was meant to bring us into God's presence and send us out changed and uplifted, you'd probably do better going to Covent Garden or even Bow Operatic Society.'

This pungent piece appeared in the Bow St Aelfric *Examiner* on Monday, the day after the installation of Vincent Stream as dean, two days before the beginning of Lent. It was read, and indeed celebrated, in and around the cathedral in a number of ways.

In the crypt office, a den of disaffection below the high altar of the cathedral, Dennis Noble, the second or canons' verger, pursed his lips in appreciation.

'Gets the flavour, wouldn't you say, Nick?'

Nick Squire, the under-verger, moved the first coffee of the day across the deal table and leaned over the older man's shoulder. He ran his eye down the column and grinned. 'To a tee. Does anyone know who writes these things?'

'That's what we'd all like to know, none more so than the new man, doubtless.' Dennis spoke as he verged, slowly, at an Anglican pace, choosing his path, choosing his words. 'Some of it could be libellous,' he remarked judiciously.

Nick pushed a plate of freshly made bacon sandwiches across the table and turned off the vent axia.

'You'll get clobbered one of these days,' said Dennis, ritualistically taking a sandwich. 'The precentor wouldn't care for it at all.'

Nick, who was well acquainted with the precentor, didn't doubt it.

'Mustard?' he inquired.

Dennis spread it as though it were holy oil. 'The precentor was put out all right,' he went on. 'You could see that. He was growling to himself all through the sermon.'

Nick nodded with pleasure at the memory. 'It doesn't augur too well for the worship side of things, does it?' he remarked, 'if the new dean can't read a service sheet?' Nick liked a row, provided it wasn't his row. He felt in this case he could afford to be detached. In six months he'd be gone for his first year at Oxford and the troubles of cathedral vergers would no longer concern him.

'Shouldn't need service sheets, deans, not if they know what they are about.' Dennis was censorious. He had high standards.

'How did Tristram take it?' There was a shade of anxiety in Nick's tone. He admired the head—the dean's—verger, and he hadn't had a chance to see him since.

'It would have been a great moment,' Dennis paced on, 'a professional peak, dean's verger verging a new dean to his pulpit for his inaugural sermon, and Dean Stream went and jumped the gun.'

Nick loved Dennis's ponderousness and wasn't above contriving moves to evoke it. 'Great moment,' he murmured.

'I'm not too sure,' said Dennis, judiciousness incarnate, 'that the ceremony was complete without a second lesson. The Holy Gospel, a proper, nay essential, part of the celebration.'

'What celebration?' asked Nick in derision. 'Nobody wanted Vincent Stream as dean, did they?'

* * *

'I really don't think it's very seemly talking about putting stoppers in decanters being like not letting you read the second lesson,' said Mrs Riddable, agitating the paper so that it flopped over the breakfast marmalade.

The parlour at the Precentory across the close from the cathedral was small. The Victorian room was taller than it was broad giving it the feeling of an upright coffin. The breakfast table took up most of the floor space and widely separated husband and wife, pinning each of them against opposite walls.

'What are you talking about?' Canon Riddable asked irritably as he extracted the Golden Shred from beneath the leaves of the *Examiner*.

'This article, this report, in the *Examiner*. About the installation of Vincent Stream. Dean Stream's installation,' his wife added, lest there should be any mistake. 'Yesterday,' she concluded.

'Oh, yes.' If Canon Riddable's tone suggested that he would prefer to know no more of the subject from his wife, he should have known better than to suppose that lack of interest on his part could quell her.

'Well, I think it's such a shame, really a *shame.*' Mrs Riddable's tone would have been suitable for reporting a case of injustice to the disabled. In physique she was a small woman, as small as her husband was large, so she put a great deal of emotion into her every utterance to make up for it. Indeed, some of her acquaintance thought she exhibited more emotion than the actual sense of her words warranted. Her short top lip and slightly protruding teeth pointed in the direction of the canon.

'Why?' asked her husband, putting down his knife and glaring across the huge length of the table.

'Because the dean's *new*,' said his wife anguishedly. 'Here,' she added. 'A stranger within our gates. We should be *welcoming* him. At the start of his ministry. Among us.'

Fifteen years of marriage had not accustomed Canon Riddable to the excesses of his wife's conversational style, nor to her habit of dividing her sentences by dramatic pauses. It always induced in him a wish to deflate her, to bring her down to face the unpleasant truths which made up, he had no doubt, the real world. He wasn't, in fact, quite sure whether she was as naive as she sounded. But he was sure that she roused in him more cynicism than was altogether proper in a residentiary canon and precentor of Bow St Aelfric Cathedral.

'I think it calls you a wizard,' his wife went

on. 'It was you who conducted the Lord Lieutenant to his pew, wasn't it?'

'I don't know what you're talking about,' said the canon shortly: 'What I do know is, there's been far too much of this pernicious anti-clerical nonsense written in that rag recently. I shall have to put a stop to it. And,' he added as an afterthought, 'Vincent Stream was an appalling choice of dean for a place like this. He's unsuitable in absolutely every conceivable way.' He found he'd raised his voice and was sweating slightly.

'Just as you say, dear,' said his wife suddenly equable, as though she had obtained the effect she wanted. A small smile slid on to her face and as quickly slid off again. 'Pass the toast, would you, Trevor?'

* * *

Stella Parish, in a Nissen hut on a piece of waste land called the Hollow three miles to the north of the cathedral, carefully unwrapped the bones and disengaged bloodstained scraps of the *Bow Examiner* from between the trotters. Her eye was caught by the name Solzhenitsyn. She'd rather liked him, she seemed to remember, way back when. Through the stains she read the rest of the paragraph. She gathered the writer hadn't thought much of the ceremony of putting in the new dean. Why exactly, she couldn't quite make out. Was it because it had been too long, or chaotically organised, or had there been a hitch in the ritual, or had the ritual been of the wrong sort, too high or too low? There was so much which could go wrong in religion, Stella reflected. It had become very complicated. She'd heard the bells on Sunday afternoon, coming across the river to the Hollow. Perhaps that had been part of the ceremony. She could just see the cathedral from the window of the hut. She wondered who the new man was: the disfigured newspaper hadn't got that bit.

As she ran her eye once more down the column of newsprint, she became aware of the black muzzle of the lurcher bitch sitting absolutely still beneath the table. A steady flow of saliva was trickling from both sides of her mouth. Stella crumpled the paper and applied a short sharp knife to the tough, fawn coloured skin of the trotter. She sliced it cleanly in half, contemplated the two halves for a moment and then pushed one over the edge of the table. Before it reached the floor, the dog's jaws took it cleanly in mid-air with a single sharp snap of tooth meeting bone.

The irregular popping of the gas flame from the cooker beneath the window recalled her to her duties. She kicked the calor gas cylinder and the gulping noises ceased to be replaced by a more reassuring continuous hiss. Stella stirred the chicken mash encouragingly. She swept her copious, dark hair back from her forehead and felt the scar running into the hair line. She thought how much of her life now revolved round feeding animals and people. Hens' mash, goats' mash, the ponies' feeds, the visitors' feeds, the community's evening meal. When she'd first come to the Hollow, three years ago, she'd felt she had nothing to offer. she'd come almost literally as a beggar with little more than the clothes she stood up in. It had been a sort of resurrection to find that there were things she could offer those who had taken her in without question or complaint. She had at least been able to cook. No, she wouldn't at all discount what she had gained. They'd helped. They'd all supported. Work had kept her sane. The animals and their demands steadied her. The rhythms of the day, week, and year, the closeness to land and weather had in time mended and healed her. Even the regularity of the trains as they swung past the Hollow gave a sort of security. There was a dangerous world out there but, protected as they were on one side by the railway and on the other by the river, the Hollow and its community were able to cultivate their virtues in tranquillity. Only now was the calm beginning to be encroached on. The building site across the field was making its way towards them. She pushed the thought from her and turned her attention to the matter in hand.

Borne on the wind with a sudden clarity, she heard the sound of the cathedral clock as it struck the hour, twelve noon. Without thinking she switched on the old wireless on the shelf above the cooker and caught the local radio station.

'This is BB Bow Broadcasting,' said the matey, demotic voice of the young commentator, 'bringing you the best in News Briefing. On Sunday . . . the crowded cathedral . . . welcomed . . . New face to this part of the world . . . well known for his work amongst the disadvantaged . . . in the great metropolis . . . Vincent Stream.'

Stella stopped stirring. She felt the familiar tightening of the stomach. Stream. He'd definitely said it. So he'd gone on, had he, Vincent Stream? Gone on and, apparently, prosperously up.

CHAPTER TWO

ILL OMENS

'Those of us who know and love back waters, whose natural habitat is the betwixt and between, will find much that is congenial about Bow St Aelfric.'

The author of the *Swallow Guide to the Cathedral Cities of England* was set to enjoy himself.

'Of the saint himself nothing is known about

his life or sanctity save only that he was slaughtered in battle with the Danes when leading a detachment of local people against them in 870. The town lies, or rather squats, for the land is marshy, in a bend of the river Bow which surrounds it on three sides. Excavations undertaken in 1922 by the then president of Bow Antiquarian Society, Sir Lionel Dunch, revealed traces of a Roman settlement with a castra and the footings of a well-built gate north of the now demolished temperance hall. Fragments of paving unearthed at that time suggest that the main Roman road to the port of Tepidunum at the mouth of the Bow must have passed near to the present site of the cathedral close. Funds ran out before the excavation could be completed and the works were filled in and not resumed. Such finds as there were are displayed in the St Aelfric Museum. The mediaeval town . . .'

The Reverend Theodora Braithwaite's attention wandered. She peered out of the carriage window at the flat, rain-swept fenland and wondered what the immediate future held in store for her. She was thirty years old, a woman in deacon's orders in the Church of England. She had set herself as part of the discipline of following a vocation properly, not to mind where she was sent nor to become too attached to any settled pattern of life. So far that attitude had resulted in a couple of years in a first curacy in east Africa followed by six months in her present curacy at St Sylvester's Betterhouse on the Thames in south-west London. There she had risen this morning in time to serve for her vicar, Geoffrey Brighouse, at his seven a.m. Eucharist in the huge Victorian Gothic church of St Sylvester. When they had finished, Geoffrey had driven her across London at a speed comparable to that which he had previously obtained from his naval helicopter. They'd shot across Southwark Bridge and hurtled down unfamiliar one-way systems of the City not yet aroused to its money-making day. Theodora, always exhilarated by Geoffrey's driving, had inquired whether he knew anything about Bow St Aelfric.

'Not a thing,' he'd replied cheerfully. 'Don't you? All those clerical ancestors of yours. Surely one of you must have bumped up against it at some time.'

Geoffrey's own family were navy. He sometimes envied Theodora who could claim descent from eight generations of Anglican clergy.

'Bow's one we missed out on,' she had said bracing herself against the seat as they swung to a halt in the forecourt of Liverpool Street station. Geoffrey had seized her bag and loped across the concourse towards the East Anglian train. Theodora followed him, bending her tall head into the evil-smelling draught which sought to repel them.

'There,' said Geoffrey, as he thrust the *Independent* into her hand. 'Should see you through as far as Grantham.'

Theodora, who would have preferred coffee, thanked him warmly and waved him away with genuine regret. She tucked it into her holdall beside her copy of this quarter's edition of *Church History Review*, settled herself in the corner seat of her empty carriage and took stock. She thought back with something like shame to the interview with the archdeacon which had brought her here. Archdeacons, Theodora reflected, are powerful people in the Anglican hierarchy. She had known a variety of them all her life. They had a say in future appointments and present comfort. Their praise or censure counted. They had the ear of bishops and were accordingly much disliked. They got used to clergy evading or resenting them. They expected flattery and the worst of them liked it. They reckond they knew what to expect in clergy attitudes so that when they met one who didn't mind too much what happened to them, and who did not, therefore, either flatter or resent, they were slow to adjust. Well, Theodora told herself, they are, after all, only human.

The archdeacon had had her into his office the day after one of his infrequent visits to the parish.

'I don't feel you're being stretched,' he'd said

jovially.

It struck Theodora that he felt she was enjoying life too much.

'Do you?' he'd inquired. But, in the manner of archdeacons, he had not stayed for an answer. He had a full diary. He could not really afford the time to listen to the views of young deacons, certainly not female ones.

He always reminded Theodora of a Victorian Shakespearian actor, bit gone to seed and rather larger than life. Over his clerical black he wore a grey woolly cardigan to disguise his real power.

'I enjoy working with Geoffrey very much,' Theodora returned cautiously.

'Of course you do,' said the archdeacon heartily. 'Super chap. Super. But we really feel you need to be stretched.'

This time the overtones of rack and thumbscrew were unmistakable.

'In a way, Theo,' the archdeacon went on, feigning intimacy (Theodora had met him only once before, and would not have dreamed of calling him 'Jim'). 'In a way,' he went on, 'all this parish stuff is pretty familiar ground to you. Your old dad and so on.'

Theodora regarded him stonily. She was damned if she was going to hear her excellent father's parochial skills patronised by this actor.

'Anyway,' he went on, 'we feel you need to branch out. A bit of experience in specialist ministries wouldn't come amiss. Widen your scope and so on. The point is,' he concluded rapidly, coming to the crux of the matter, 'the bishop's been asked to supply someone to do a couple of months on adult lay training, pastoral assistants, readers, that sort of thing. The laity are very important, you know.'

Theodora, who did not doubt it, and had no objection at all to extending her knowledge in that area, nevertheless felt it only fair to point out that she had no experience.

'Precisely,' the archdeacon grinned like a shark. 'Just my point.'

'When?' inquired Theodora.

'Start Monday.'

'Lent starts on Wednesday,' she pointed out just in case the archdeacon might have overlooked this. It would certainly be inconvenient for poor Geoffrey to work the parish suddenly deprived of his curate.

But the archdeacon had his own priorities and the convenience of a newish, youngish vicar who looked as though he were going to be too efficient by half, was not one of them. 'Theo,' the archdeacon pushed his elbow across the desk and threw his bulk after it. He lowered his voice a couple of octaves. 'Theo,' he repeated, 'no one is indispensable. That's a bit of pastoral advice I can give you out of thirty years' experience.'

His voice, which had been the making of him, gave unassailable authority to this banality.

'On your bike, pastures new, eh?' he said cheerfully, rising to his feet and, therefore, drawing Theodora after him.

'Where?'

'What?'

'Where am I going?'

'Oh, didn't I say? Bow. Bow St Aelfric. I expect you know it, with all your clerical connexions,' he added maliciously. 'Actually,' he went on, his real interests shining through for a moment, 'it's architecturally odd. It's got two towers, one over the crossing and one over the west end. The monks of the original foundation built the crossing one, the townspeople built the other because they couldn't stand the monks. So they put up a partition wall and each group worshipped separately for about two hundred years. Back to back. Paradigm of the Christian life,' he concluded, truth gaining hold of him. 'I think they've just put in their new dean. Vincent Stream. Not perhaps an ideal choice,' he could not refrain from adding, 'but certainly an interesting one.' He returned to his former tack. 'Lots of challenges. God bless.'

So here she was on a bitter Monday morning in the week of Ash Wednesday, bound for St Aelfric, to which, though she had failed to convince the archdeacon of it, she looked forward. The archdeacon was right, it would enlarge her scope, there might be all sorts of exciting things in store.

She resumed her study of the *Swallow Guide* and gazed from time to time out of the window at the fleeing landscape. They must be nearing journey's end. The countryside ceased to be a flat, dyke-measured fenland and gave way to a patchwork of market gardens. Chicken wire flapped loose and dangerous in the prevailing east wind. Cabbages, monstrous growths like small trees, ran to seed in allotments beside the bypass. Bungalows thickened, the hangars housing light industry began to close in. Theodora gazed over the last remaining hedges. The carriages swung round a bend and in the distance the double towers of Bow St Aelfric Cathedral rose above the office blocks.

A moment later Theodora's eye lighted upon a cluster of caravans and Nissen huts. From one of these parked close to the railway line a woman emerged and began to hang out clothes. The train slowed for a moment and Theodora had the uncanny experience, sometimes afforded by train journeys, of staring straight into the eyes of someone who could not possibly be looking back at her. She glimpsed a face, haggard by too much experience, the mouth wide and generous, copious brown hair swept back from the brow and streaked with rain. There was a scar on the forehead, she noticed, running into the hair line. A moment later the train hooted in triumph and stormed into Bow St Aelfric station.

* * *

The grandest house in the cathedral close was the Deanery. The plain eighteenth-century stone façade stared at the cathedral across the perfectly kept green sward, with a certain worldly insolence. It at least did not have to pretend that it was anything other than what it was, a gentleman's residence.

In his study on the first floor, the newly installed dean raised his gaze from the day-book on the desk and allowed his eye to stay on the glass of the window. It was the original bottle glass and therefore opaque. It was, moreover, he noticed with irritation, streaked with dust. Nothing in this place worked. The whole house needed redecorating. The cellars had flooded a week ago with the March rains. The smell from the inundation seemed to linger still. Cracks in the drawing-room walls suggested there might be problems with subsidence. He would have to take steps. Taking steps was what he was good at, what he had been put into Bow St Aelfric to do.

Vincent Stream had fixed his priorities early in life. As a schoolboy he had gazed in at the lighted windows of Father Cuthbert's tall house in Bodium Crescent in Birkenhead. On winter evenings, which was how he remembered it, a single immense table lamp had illuminated the study. Sombre book backs glowed, heavy curtains framed the windows. Leather armchairs and oil paintings could be glimpsed from beyond the railings which set the house apart from the street. Vincent had loitered on the rain-swept pavement and decided that that was how he would like to live. He wanted nothing to do with his father's brick semi up the Liverpool bypass. He had fallen in love with a set of artifacts. He but partly understood what was attracting him.

'Do you believe in God?' he'd asked his pinafored mother one evening on his return home. His father, who was reading *The Amateur Gardener*, put it down and looked at his son. 'Don't be cheeky to your mother,' he said without rancour, mild, excellent man that he was.

His mother had placed the liver and bacon on the oilclothed table and bidden him wash his hands. It had all been very ordinary.

Father Cuthbert's lighted window had guided Vincent as truly as more refined visions had guided the early saints. It worked upon his emotions. It irradiated his life. He would be a priest and live like a gentleman. He'd have a house that other people would stare into with envy. He'd have a study. It would be lined with books and have soft lights and oils over the fireplace. He longed, he thirsted to live differently from his parents. He plotted his path.

Undistinguished in intellect, he was, nevertheless, prepared to put in more hours than his classmates at what his mother called book work. In adolescence, while his contemporaries were experimenting with the delights of cars and girls, he was upstairs in his bedroom doing his prep. He hung on by the skin of his teeth to the Latin set at his grammar school. When his voice broke, he found himself blessed with a serviceable baritone and on the strength of it joined St Augustine's church choir. Thus placed, he could study the habits and mannerisms of the clergy whom he learned to call high church. He imitated their southern vowels and listened attentively to their careful, doctrinal sermons. The real presence, the seven sacraments, the importance of the eastward position became important to him because they were invested with emotion by those whom he sought to emulate. God, when he came to him, came in the form of a rather taller and mistier Father Cuthbert. Father Cuthbert did not possess a beard, but perhaps God did, Vincent thought.

Father Cuthbert, an aesthete, a politician, well born, well heeled from his grandfather's cotton mills, had two curates and a social standing in Birkenhead. He did not especially like Vincent. He'd had better looking, better bred and more intelligent lads through his hands, but he knew his duty when presented with tenacity of the kind discernible in Stream.

When Vincent sought his advice about a vocation and a university place, Father Cuthbert, an Oxford man, had declared that they took anyone for theology at Cambridge. His parents, hesitant but overawed by the presence of the priest, revised their feelings that their boy would do very nicely with a course in geography at Reading, and gave way. And so it had proved.

Three years at Selwyn had brought him nearer to the study and its soft lights, the books and the envied window, the lives he wanted to follow and join. He wasted not a minute of his time at Cambridge, made his friends and doggedly won his respectable degree.

Theological college had been followed by a single curacy in Halifax, appalling enough to convince him that he had no talent for pastoral work in a parish. He did not care for the poor. They and their houses smelt. He did not like their children; their directness, his inability to impress them frightened him. He liked well-dressed, prosperous adults with southern vowels. That was what he'd joined the church for, to mix with nice people. It was not that he doubted that Christianity was for all people. He did think that. That is what the church had taught him. But he felt there should be order in it. The flowing of one category into another, priest into layman, high into low, was a difficulty, for him. He liked clear boundaries, order and predictability, above all, a secure unarguable social place for himself. Over the years he had studied the trappings of priesthood, loved them and adopted them. He had made himself an expert on the accoutrements of clerical gentility.

After the disastrous first curacy, he'd looked around for something, anything, which would guarantee him a position he did not have to make himself, where he could depend on other people's expectations to see him through. He'd been fortunate. He thanked Providence. A Cambridge friend who had been appointed to a chaplaincy at a provincial university got jaundice at the last minute. Before disappearing into hospital he mentioned Vincent to the bishop. Vincent made sure he never had to look back. He'd worked hard and systematically. He had a modest talent for organisation. He knew about dates, could read a balance sheet, genuinely liked male Christian students who took him at his face value. He made a moderate success. A first chaplaincy was followed in due course by a second at a more illustrious university. He'd been industrious and published in the not too intellectually demanding pages of *Theology*. Incapable of original thought, he had hit upon the idea of editing collections of other people's work, men more gifted than himself. His abilities for taking pains, checking footnotes, keeping the dilatory up to publication dates, found their proper métier. In time, with no research or original work to his credit, he had gained the reputation within the church of being a competent scholar. And, as the standards of the Church of England went at that time, so did he feel himself to be. 'Dedicated' was an epithet often attached to his name. To what, few bothered to inquire. In his sermons he learned to mix sound Catholic doctrine with reference to the modernly fashionable. If the two bits didn't always cohere, few were capable of noticing.

Twenty years after that first chaplaincy, the deanery of Bow St Aelfric had been his reward. In the course of his careful efforts, he'd made himself useful to a handful of bishops who felt they ought to have a publication to their name. He'd entertained one or two Christian MPs and the odd permanent secretary. When St Aelfric came up, the tall crown appointment secretary had looked at the short crown appointment secretary and nodded. It had been done. The phone calls had been made, the soundings taken. The committee met, but it was mere form. All had already been decided. Six months later Vincent Stream had heard the fanfare and processed to his dean's stall. A lesser man, as he sank into the velvet cushions, might have thought he had achieved all that could be expected and more. But Dean Stream had looked across at the bishop's throne and knew there was one more step along the road to go.

Hence his feverish activity over the last few weeks. The moment he put down the phone call confirming his appointment Stream had written to the suffragan bishop, Henry Clement, who was also vice-dean and a residentiary canon of Bow Cathedral. The long tenure of the last dean, urged to his retirement in his eighties and dead soon after, would mean there was a lot to do. 'No one was more admiring of Dean Mantle's work for the cathedral over the last half century,' Stream had written in his own small neat handwriting, but he was eager to get to grips with the tasks which lay ahead. Would chapter allow him to come down a month before his installation to make a start on the in-tray?

The suffragan bishop showed the letter to the diocesan bishop. The relations between a cathedral chapter and the bishop of the diocese are delicate. In theory the dean and chapter are entirely independent of the bishop but in fact long-established bishops usually have their cathedral's chapters well in hand. They have, after all, appointed at least some of their members.

A thruster, thought the diocesan bishop, Ronald Holdall, when he read the letter. But he didn't dislike the idea. He was looking forward to doing a bit less in his final couple of years. He'd accepted an invitation to the States and was busy soliciting another from India. It would be convenient to have someone capable in the cathedral and politic for him to withdraw for a month or to while the new man found his feet with the chapter. 'Tell him he can come, and square Riddable and Gold,' he'd said naming the two other residentiary canons, the first of whom was precentor, the second archdeacon. The suffragan had, therefore, written a cordial note to Stream assuring him he'd be most welcome to come down prior to his installation.The courtesies exchanged, the goal posts agreed, Vincent Stream had come. He had spent a day looking through the files. It had been every bit as appalling as he had hoped. Nothing had been done for at least twenty years. Finance, fabric, furniture, personnel and liturgy were all a neglected shambles. Here if anywhere a name could be made. It was God's gift.

Now, on the Monday morning after his installation, he could begin work in earnest. On the desk beside the day-book lay a copy of the service sheet for his installation. The dean's mouth tightened. There was the place to start his reforms. He would need to restore proper Catholic worship to a cathedral which could put on something as shambolic as his installation. Neither clergy nor vergers had the least idea how to comport themselves reverently on such an occasion. The dean's verger should have stopped him going ahead too promptly. It had been a farce. He brought the face of the man into focus. He hadn't cared for him when he'd first met him. He dressed too well and he behaved as though he had a private income. He was too familiar. He shifted uneasily in his chair. He'd bide his time and then sack him. And the other one he'd need to ease out would be Erica Millhaven. God save us. *A female canon. A female residentiary* canon.

He pulled his day-book towards him. It had a worn leather cover and a single page diary which he renewed every year. Tucked into the front pocket was a manuscript. He looked again at the compliments slip fixed to it by a paper clip. It said, '*Church History Review* ed. I. Markewicz'. Then in a strong hand, 'Would very much value your opinion on this in the not too distant future.' Well he had made his views perfectly clear in that quarter. As for Archdeacon Gold, he would do as he was told. And the first thing he needed to be told was how to dress. Clerical dress was only fair on the laity. They needed to be able to recognise a priest. Yesterday he'd seen Gold in track suit and trainers jogging through the close.

That, thought the dean, left the local community. The article in the *Bow Examiner* was so painful he could hardly bear to read it. Who on earth had written it? What on earth possessed them to publish it? He wasn't familiar enough as yet with the local scene to know whom to approach to get this sort of thing stopped. He'd ask the suffragan and see if he knew. His eye went down the column again. 'What is a cathedral for?' he read. He'd teach them what a cathedral was for. Bow St Aelfric, which had towers that symbolised the division of clergy and laity and the insolence of the laity towards the clergy, would find out what a cathedral was for. That quality, that schism symbolised in the cathedral's very architecture was an affront. It was a pity they could not pull one of the towers down but at least there would be no doubt in future about where leadership and authority lay. The only difficulty was the quality of the troops.

He peered at the window again and this time his eye managed to penetrate the opacity and streaks of dust and rain. Below him, crossing the close, he observed the tall figure of the suffragan bishop, his ear courteously inclined to the stocky archdeacon who trotted beside him. The dean picked up the internal phone, newly installed, a symbol of his intentions. Communications, he'd learned on his first management course, are vitally important.

'Mrs Perfect,' he addressed his secretary at her desk in the cathedral office, at right angles to the Deanery, 'contact the suffragan and the archdeacon for me and say I'd like to see them both at eleven forty-five here. And bring up my file on finance.' Vincent Stream never said please or thank you in contexts like this. He'd been surprised initially, but had in time come to accept, how very impressed people were by an omission of these usual courtesies.

'Yes, Mr Dean. Oh, Mr Dean, you're due to see Canon Millhaven and Miss Braithwaite at twelve.'

'Cancel them,' said Vincent levelly.

Crouched over her typewriter, Mrs Perfect pursed her lips at her colleague, Miss Current. 'That's what they call prioritising.'

* * *

The taxi carrying Theodora from Bow station seemed to have lost its way. It had started off confidently in what looked the right direction for the city but had then been thrown off course by roadworks. The diversion signs had given out some time ago. It began to rain with the cold determination of March in East Anglia.

Theodora looked at her watch. Eleven o'clock. She was due to meet Canon Millhaven at eleven thirty and the Dean at twelve. She didn't care to be late, ever, and especially not when meeting senior clergy for the first time. She leaned forward to make contact with the driver. She had framed, 'How much further?' when she noticed the deaf aid in his ear. She sank back defeated. The roadworks continued. Mechanical diggers pitted themselves against piles of rubble. Pumps sucked and excreted turbid water from one flooded trench to another. Huge fissures in the tarmac gave the impression that the whole area had suffered some convulsion and was sinking into the abyss. Perhaps being built on a fen meant a continuous battle to keep above water. Perhaps she was doomed to continue for eternity being driven between mounds of bitter-smelling earth and deracinated paving stones by a deaf driver with the rain pounding on the roof of the car. Perhaps the end of the world was at hand. At that moment, the cab rounded a cluster of JCBs, the rain ceased and the Cathedral of Bow St Aelfric rose up before her.

The oddity of the double towers, monuments to the hostility of clergy and laity, was apparent. The cathedral had not in fact been built in the nineteenth century but it looked as though it had. The Victorian restoration of the entire buildings by Sir Giles Gilbert Scott at the height of his powers overbore anything which the thirteenth-century craftsmen had originally intended. The band of saints and prophets who strode round the west front at clerestory level had had their robes tidied up and recut and their facial expressions etherialised by masons who knew what men of God ought to look like.

The building rose out of a sea of traffic. A carefully thought out one-way system ensured that articulated lorries ground in low gear past the west front day and night. The north side was buttressed by a solid phalanx of cars in the car park serving the magistrates' courts. Not very often could the bells of the cathedral be heard through the roar of engines.

Before Theodora could further contemplate the setting, the taxi swung under an archway to the south of the cathedral. The roar of traffic vanished as though switched off. The contrast with the street outside was absolute. Theodora took in a wide stretch of grass enclosed on three sides by domestic buildings and on the fourth by the cathedral's south side. Only a nifty piece of real estate dealing by the last archdeacon but one had preserved the close from the machinations of planners. 'People expect a bit of tranquillity in the middle of all this chaos,' he had remarked, surveying the moderate traffic of the mid-1930s. Later generations had had cause for gratitude.

'Where to?' The deaf driver jerked his head in interrogation.

'This'll do very nicely,' said Theodora.

'What?'

Theodora followed the notices marked 'Cathedral Office' into a building which parodied the cathedral, all pointed windows and Victorian Gothic turrets, at right angles to the handsome eighteenth-century stone building which she remarked on the other side of the close. A moment or two later, as she passed from office to archway, Theodora glanced up. She caught sight of a tall figure framed in the window of the room over the arch. Canon Millhaven, Theodora conjectured and ascended the narrow wooden staircase which would take her into her presence.

In her office over the Archgate Canon Erica Millhaven wrestled with the sash window. It gave in suddenly in the manner of the recalcitrant and flew up, catching Canon Millhaven off balance. The rain had stopped and a hesitant sun was breaking through the grey scudding clouds. She pushed the lower half of the casement open to its fullest extent, positioned herself in front of it and breathed in deeply and slowly. Standing in the open doorway Theodora gazed with interest at the various bits of Canon Millhaven's anatomy which threatened to be displayed by this exercise. She felt a moment's apprehension lest she should be forced to see parts of the canon which would be better covered. Erica Millhaven relied, Theodora feared, too much on safety pins.

Canon Millhaven was a rare breed in the Anglican Church. There were one or two female honorary canons in various advanced dioceses but residentiary ones, responsible for the worship and ministry of cathedrals, members of chapters and with stalls in the choir, these were still few and far between. Recent legislation had only just made it possible for women in deacon's orders to be appointed to such a position. Her preferment had made the national press, or any way, the

Church Times, which, in its liberal way, had welcomed it.

That had been a year ago. Canon Millhaven was into her sixties and within striking distance of retirement. Age had not much dimmed her energy, that wide-ranging and frightening vigour, that enthusiasm for work on what she called in her penetrating voice, the frontiers of the Church's ministry. There were a fair number of people who simply could not stand Canon Millhaven. Others felt she was well worth the gate money.

Canon Millhaven dabbed her finger in the puddles on the outside windowledge.

'It comes from God,' she exclaimed, gesturing to the remains of the weather and moving towards her desk.

Theodora agreed.

'It bloweth where it listeth, the Holy Spirit,' she went on emphatically as though the weather and the Holy Spirit might be connected.

Theodora agreed. Canon Millhaven tapped a newspaper on her desk. 'We are not loved, and while we resist the Spirit we should not expect to be.'

Theodora had no idea what she was talking about. 'We cannot and should not attempt to predict its operancy,' Canon Millhaven went on.

Theodora resisted the temptation to agree. She waited.

Canon Millhaven swung round to eye her. 'That is the commonest mistake of the Church at this present hour,' she said severely.

'Perhaps, indeed, at any time,' Theodora advanced mildly. She had no objection to discussing theology with anyone but felt it should always be informed by an historical perspective. Aware, however, that Canon Millhaven was thirty years older than she and doubtless familiar with the biblical evidence for her unexceptional point of view, she held her tongue.

'Now is the day of salvation,' said Canon Millhaven as though someone had contradicted her.

Theodora wondered how much longer she was going to be exposed to this barrage of theological clichés.

As though aware of her unspoken thought, Miss Millhaven gathered her billowing shawl about her shoulders and moved to the far side of her desk. She was a tall, well-formed woman, her hair, thick and nearly white, was cut to ear length. Her eyes, light grey and rather prominent, were set wide apart above a strongly modelled nose and jaw. Her complexion and demeanour radiated health. She sat down, bent her head for a moment as though about to say a grace, raised it again to meet Theodora's own level gaze, and smiled. Then she began to be detailed, exact and efficient about the training of laymen in the diocese of St Aelfric. It was as though there were two different people present in one body. Theodora in her turn ceased to be a spectator and became involved and responsive.

They were both so immersed that the sound of the cathedral clock striking twelve noon took them by surprise. Canon Millhaven stopped in mid-sentence, raised her head and, like the Queen of the Willis at the crack of dawn, almost visibly cocked her ear.

'We are due at the dean's,' she said rising. At that moment the telephone shrilled. Canon Millhaven regarded it for a second as though uncertain what its purpose might be. Then, raising the head-piece to her ear, she said in a surprisingly high voice, 'Yes?'

There was a moment's silence, then, 'And did he offer an alternative time? ... I see. Thank you, Mrs Perfect.'

She turned to Theodora. 'The dean has cancelled. I regret the discourtesy.'

Theodora murmured deprecatingly.

'We need new blood here, Miss Braithwaite. We decay, we grow rancid. New blood, I say.' Canon Millhaven went on. 'But whether as transfusion or sacrifice, I do not pretend to know.'

CHAPTER THREE

THEOPHANY

In the cathedral close, Rebecca Riddable bounced the ball expertly against the green and white painted notice which said 'No Ball Games'. The sign was an impressive one. It resembled a triple, Lorraine cross. The top piece bore the interdict on ball games. Beneath that was a second, longer arm which said, 'Keep Off The Grass'. Below that was another short one which said 'No Dogs'. Beneath this last had been added in small, very neat italic script, 'What shall we do to be saved?' The 'shall' had been underlined. In the watery sunlight the three children had been bouncing the ball at the notice for twenty minutes. There were neat, round mud marks between each of the words.

'Why aren't you at school?' Mrs Perfect inquired of the young Riddables as she crossed the close on her return from lunch.

'We've had mumps,' said Rebecca smugly. She expected to be able to quell people and was evolving, for a twelve year old, a good armoury of weapons for this purpose. Her mother's daughter, she knew that making people feel guilty was a sure way of asserting superiority. Mumps meant being ill. Being ill meant suffering. Those who suffered were blessed. It said so in the Bible, one Peter three fourteen.

'Well, I shouldn't let your father catch you,' said Mrs Perfect. unwilling to be bested and reckoning she was on to a good move.

'He's not here. He's out in the sticks chasing up an incumbent,' said the youngest boy.

'You shouldn't say it like that, Ben,' his sister admonished. 'You should always say, he's at a meeting.'

'Or burying the dead,' the middle boy chimed in. 'Or marrying the ...' He stopped puzzled. 'What do you marry like you bury the dead?' A stolid ten year old, the middle one in a family of three, he liked there to be symmetry in language as in life.

Mrs Perfect hadn't an answer to this so she contented herself with saying, 'Well, I expect he wouldn't like the notice damaged,' and dashed for the office door before they could entangle her further. She could see why people were afraid of children. Their questions seemed to want to unhinge the world, to cut it adrift from its normal moorings. They were always peering down side roads which common sense and adulthood would tell them were best left unexplored.

A big woman, and light on her feet, she raced upstairs. The staircase gave immediately on to a large space used as a waiting room. Its function was clear from two potted plants, not in the best of health, a couple of padded chairs and a photostat machine. No one had had an office big enough to accommodate this last item, except the archdeacon or Canon Riddable. Clearly neither of those could be expected to house it, so it had been placed in this no man's land until they could think what to do with it. At first it hadn't been much used. The ambitions of a diocesan secretary had landed them with it. When he had gone on to higher things, there'd been a move to get rid of it. But as time went on its functions had grown on people. It became, if not a facilitator of office efficiency, at least a boost to social life. There was no common-room, so typists took their morning coffees and afternoon teas round it. Its presence provided an excuse for the overworked to snatch a brief respite from the keyboard.

At the moment it had a client. The suffragan bishop gazed at the instrument before him. It looked to him like a cross between a fridge and a television. He could open a fridge, he knew and, also, though less often, he had been known successfully to switch off a television set. Now, however, he was flummoxed. There were, he calculated, eleven different buttons which he might press. He was spoilt for choice. Which one would render it his servant? He jabbed with no great confidence at a medium-sized square button in the middle of the row. Nothing happened. He paused to regroup. Then, greatly daring, he pushed the biggest orange coloured button. There was a whirring sound and the cassette to his left jumped from its bed and hit the floor scattering A4 over a wide area.

Mrs Perfect moved swiftly forward. 'May I help you, Bishop?

The bishop turned a smile of enormous sweetness upon her. His fine-boned features, all interesting planes and points, like a Rodin bronze, radiated gratitude. His ability not merely to look helpless but actually to be so, had stood him in good stead all his professional life. The good willed, especially amongst the laity, flocked to help him. He had no pride, no shame. He knew (and the more sophisticated of his rescuers knew) that he did them a kindness in allowing them scope for their charity. 'He's scarcely competent to open a door,' Mrs Perfect had exclaimed to Miss Current recently as she slit open four letters he had sealed himself to check that he'd managed to match content to address. (He hadn't.)

'Bishops quite often don't *have* to open doors for themselves,' Miss Current had reflected.

'They get out of practice,' Mrs Perfect had gone on. 'Then when he does have to struggle with one, he traps his fingers. But he's a good man,' she concluded. 'Always says please and thank you.'

Mrs Perfect gathered the scattered leaves, opened the flap and took his handwritten manuscript from his unresisting hand. 'How many copies?' she asked soothingly.

'Copies? Oh, yes. The dean, Canon Millhaven, Miss er Braithwaite. That's er ...'

'Three,' said Mrs Perfect setting the dial. The machine gave a satisfied grunting noise and out came the copies. The bishop expressed his warm gratitude.

Mrs Perfect gathered up the copies and stowed them carefully in an envelope from the pile on the shelf. Then she looked back at the trays.

'Is this one of yours, Bishop? ' she inquired.

The bishop regarded the typescript in amazement. Did these machines produce original documents? He took it cautiously and scanned the heading.

It said, 'A View from a Pew'. It sounded familiar. He began to read.

'No,' he said firmly. 'It does not belong to me.' Absently he tucked it into his own papers.

* * *

Theodora met the suffragan as he descended the stairs. She was faced with the usual dilemma of such occasions. She stood back to give him passage because he was a bishop and she was a curate in deacon's orders. The bishop in his turn stood back because he was a gentleman whose manners predated any revision by feminism. She let him have his way and gained the waiting room. She surveyed the décor, pitied the plants and, eschewing the chairs, made for the notice board on the far wall. It held two curling postcards from well-attended resorts in Spain and Greece and an advertisement for a pilgrimage to the Holy Land for the Easter before last. Pinned above these was a minatory notice about smoking and a copy of the cathedral's services for the current week, the week of Ash Wednesday, the beginning of Lent. Theodora was pleased to see there was a daily eight o'clock Eucharist and Compline on Wednesdays and Fridays. The canon in residence for the month was someone called Canon Trevor Riddable.

She was due to meet Archdeacon Archibald Gold at two-thirty. It was twenty past two and they'd said, downstairs, he was not yet back from lunch. She settled herself to wait.

After the dean's phone call, Canon Millhaven had terminated her session with Theodora and pointed her in the direction of the cathedral guest flat.

The flat had proved to be two rooms with a tiny kitchen and shower at the top of the house next to the cathedral office. The living room looked as though no one had touched it since the last, clerical, owner had vacated it round about 1870. In the kitchen, however, the fridge had provided milk, the cupboard bread, marmite and coffee. She'd made what she considered an excellent lunch. Things immediately looked brighter. She had consulted her timetable. Canon Millhaven had provided a very full programme of work for the next fortnight, remarking that she had better start by seeing everything they were doing. They were doing a great deal. Theodora had packed an ordnance survey map of the surrounding country and a street plan of the town just in case the archdeacon got technical.

Theodora looked again round the desolate waiting room which served both the general office and Archdeacon Gold's. It was going to be like this for some days, she reflected, waiting for people, making arrangements, feeling disorientated, not knowing which engagements were going to be important or, for that matter, which new acquaintance. Fits and starts. Betwixt and betweens. Half landings and outdated notices. She recognised in herself a deep love of routine; a dependable rhythm of work and prayer was her ideal. Was it a fault, she wondered. In theory she held one should depend on nothing, expect nothing, be continually open to the prompting of the Spirit. In reality she would prefer to be able to predict, to know where she stood.

She cast her eye round the room in search of occupation and lit upon the *Bow Examiner* lodged beside the dying plant. Theodora was addicted to the provincial press. It seemed to her that they had a more wholesome set of interests than the nationals and treated their material more imaginatively. She had spent many a happy moment with accounts of the Royal Norfolk show or the Frostbites' under-fifteens dinghy trials in the columns of the *Eastern Daily Press.*

She turned to the middle pages and read the article under the heading of 'A View from a Pew'. Was this what Canon Millhaven had meant this morning when she had tapped a newspaper on her desk and said the church had no right to be loved? Theodora glanced at it again. It was signed 'A. Pathfinder' which was presumably a *nom de plume*. The writing was passionate. It was composed, she judged, by someone who was knowledgeable, who cared deeply about the Anglican Church and who felt that the least it could do was to get its rituals right. Well, given the immense privileges of the cathedral clergy, so they should, Theodora ruminated. She wondered though at a local newspaper printing anything so critical. What lay behind it? Was it part of a policy, part of a long-running feud?

She was recalled from her speculations by the sound of voices from the hall below.

'Your questions are impertinent. I have no intention of answering them.' The voice was high, the accent clipped, the tone irritable. The voice which answered was lower. Theodora couldn't make out the words. The first voice resumed. 'Moreover, you're a nuisance, Fresh. You're not a scholar and you have no qualifications which give you any right to go around pontificating about the fabric of the cathedral. In particular, I shall not permit you to meddle with the alterations which I intend to make to the west door.'

This time Theodora could distinguish the reply.

'You see,' the other man was explaining patiently, 'the very site here is an ancient and sacred one. It's much older than Christianity. A building as old as the cathedral isn't an artifact, a plaything for any old committee of amateurs. It's more like a piece of the natural world, a forest or landscape. A serious house on serious earth.' The voice had a slight local accent and the words though spoken more slowly than his interlocutor's were passionately urged.

'The ordering of the cathedral is the responsibility of the dean and chapter and of no one else.'

The lower voice tried to interrupt but was overridden by the higher one. 'I am not going to argue with you further. You're an autodidact, too ignorant to know what that word means. I shall proceed as I think best.'

The voice had become more audible as its owner's footsteps ascended the stairs. Theodora thought it politic to become very interested in the advertisement for last year's trip to the Holy Land. She was not unfamiliar with the manners of senior clergy but, even so, she was surprised at the tone of the conversation. The owner of the voice, square of head and square of figure, attired in deep clerical black with a narrow clerical collar, marched past her, without a glance, into the general office.

She leaned over the banisters to see if she could see the other party to the unequal conversation. There was no one in the hall below but the door to the close was open and the figure of a man could be seen receding through it.

Theodora was cheered by this episode. She felt that she was beginning to build up local knowledge. What further would she be offered? The cathedral clock struck the half hour. The archdeacon arrived on cue. The downstairs door slammed. There was a lot of noisy stamping. Then a bulky figure in leather jacket, rain pouring from every part of it, stamped up the stairs. He wore what might have been a flying helmet and carried a pair of gauntlets in one hand and a canvas holdall in the other. He began unzipping odd bits of attire and from beneath the layers emerged a tweed-suited figure rather smaller than might have been supposed from his outer cladding. Theodora judged him to be in his middle forties. Nature had grouped the archdeacon's features in the middle of his face and then allowed them to slide down to rest on a powerful looking moustache which, as it were, ruled them off. His thin reddish hair was sleeked thriftily from a low parting over the dome of his head. This he turned in Theodora's direction.

'Shan't be a mo,' he said and disappeared through the door marked 'Gentlemen'.

The archdeacon's office, when she entered it, looked like a store room into which detritus from other offices and parts of the cathedral had been piled. There were bits of a dismantled pulpit propped against one wall. Perched on a cupboard behind the desk a couple of marble cherubs' heads in the Italian taste smiled happily down either side of the archdeacon's own head. Chairs, plastic, canvas and bentwood, were piled in every corner and what looked like parts of an outboard motor rendered the floor as dangerous as a minefield. The archdeacon bounded nimbly over them and gained his desk in safety. He flung himself down in his revolving chair which promptly tipped backwards with his weight. He hooked his legs on to his desk as though to secure himself in place. Theodora found herself addressed by an almost recumbent figure.

'I'm sorry I haven't got terribly much time. I'm up to my eyes.'

Theodora murmured about how very understandable this was. She thought how often she had sat on chairs in front of other people's desks. Were desks necessary? Her eye lit on the perfect miniature of a Rolls Royce

Silver Ghost 1925 mounted on a wooden base which took up a good part of the archdeacon's desk. She brought her attention back to the archdeacon. His cuffs, she noticed, were secured by very large, gold links. His watch was likewise in a chunky gold bracelet. He was not wearing a clerical collar.

'Just one or two points.' The archdeacon stopped to marshal his thoughts. 'Erica's fixed you with digs et cetera?'

Theodora nodded. She could see she wasn't expected to talk.

'Right. Right. Got a TT?' He cast round the muddle of papers on his desk and whilst retaining his recumbent position extracted a sheet. 'We're delighted you could come and help us out. Of course. Growth area.' He appeared to have got a grip on the business in hand. 'Children's work in the parish. The junior church. The young unchurched.'

'Adult lay education,' Theodora said cautiously.

'That too.' The archdeacon's eye glazed as he sought for his cliché. 'Words like "outreach" and "mission" are integral to the chapter's vision for the church in this diocese,' he said rapidly. 'We're looking,' he leaned forward as far as he could without actually compromising his horizontal hold, 'for a far more aggressive interchange between parish and diocese. We're looking for renewal on every front.'

There was an almighty crash. The office seemed to rock slightly. Somewhere outside a woman shrieked. There was a sound of running feet. The archdeacon hesitated, then disengaged his feet from his desk and hauled himself upright. Once on his feet he gained courage and impetus. 'Something's up,' he said acutely. 'Half a mo.'

They moved swiftly down the stairs. Outside the rain had started again. It was slanting evilly across the close in teaming rods. It was difficult to see. The quiet which Theodora had noticed on her first entry to the close before lunch had given way to a pandemonium of noise. Doors slammed. There was a deep sound of drumming which might have been running feet or running water. Through it all came the high stomach churning wail of a child frightened or in pain. The archdeacon sprinted towards the middle of the green sward at a pace which suggested he jogged regularly. Theodora followed with long strides.

Where the notice board had stood half an hour before was a crater about three feet wide and six feet long.

From one end water mixed with mud and shingle was gushing with some force. The board swayed to and fro in the current. At the far end of the hole a girl of about eleven was kneeling and peering into the crater. Beside her, clinging to her coat, was a younger child, a boy. It was his cry which was filling the air.

There was a smell of ancient earth and wet stone.

'What happened?' panted the archdeacon to the girl.

Theodora bent over the crater. Her eyes met those of another small boy sitting on the floor, his hair plastered to his round head, mud caking his anorak.

'I'm all right, I think. It was rather a surprise,' he said courteously in answer to Theodora's inquiry. Theodora extended a hand. He lodged his foot on the side of the hole, braced his weight against it and allowed himself to be hoisted up.

Behind Theodora a small interested crowd was gathering. Mrs Perfect, a plastic mackintosh over her head, was taking charge of the two other children. A man in dungarees straddled the hole and engaged the archdeacon in conversation about the probable source of the water-flow. Tourists who found present events more fascinating than ancient architecture were beginning to gather. One young man slid to the front. He was hailed by Mrs Perfect as 'Nick' and told to ring the fire brigade. The young man slid off again. At that moment a small figure thrust its way with competent elbows through the crowd.

'Rebecca,' declared Mrs Riddable, flinging her arm round her eldest child who did not move away. 'Benjamin,' she exclaimed to her youngest. He obligingly clung in Victorian set-piece fashion to her skirts. Her attempts to envelop Timothy were less physically successful. She lacked a third arm and he for his part, was extremely muddy and seemed to feel this disqualified him from too close a contact. He was, in any case, reluctant to divorce himself completely from the fissure behind him.

'I'm all right,' he said firmly. Then he turned to Theodora. 'Hadn't we better get the other one out?'

'What?' said the archdeacon.

'Where?' said his mother.

'Who?' said Theodora.

Timothy gestured back into the hole. The crowd took a step forward. At that moment the rain ceased. A sudden brilliant shaft of cold March sun slanted directly into the pit. At the bottom, rising from the mud and shingle, as though struggling to free itself from a grave in which it had been interred, could be seen the form of a body cut off at the waist.

There was a moment's silence. Then with a nimble movement, one of the bystanders slipped into the hole and began to scrape away at the shape. Gradually a hunched figure could be made out.

'There,' said Oliver Fresh, brushing the last of the mud from the shallow eye sockets of the idol. 'I told you so, didn't I?' He looked up in triumph at the archdeacon. The Roman god Janus stared up at them out of the pit in which he had lain for sixteen hundred years.

* * *

'So what happened?' Stella Parish asked Oliver Fresh as she chopped onions on the kitchen table in the hut in the Hollow.

Fresh removed his head from beneath the cold tap. It was a large, well shaped head covered with black curling hair and a full, neatly trimmed beard from which grey eyes and red lips emerged sparkling with life. The head was crafted, wrought, not unlike an artifact which might have been dug up or have decorated a pre-Norman building. One of the many people who did not care for Fresh had once compared him to a tadpole for his head was large in comparison to his neat slim body. Stella, who had started off by finding him slightly repulsive had come, over the three years of her own stay at the Hollow, to love him. He was physically dexterous. She had watched his long tapering hands and seen how at home they were with materials of all kinds, how he formed them, caressed them, worked them.

His workshop, which led off the living part of the hut they shared, was clean and neat with tools of different crafts hung on different parts of the wall. She had learned to recognise the implements of metal work, wood work, stone work, gem cutting and leather working. Down the middle of the room ran a long table fitted with clamps and a lathe. The whole place smelt of wood, oil and leather. At the far end was a single bunk in which Fresh slept. Over it was a shelf of books: Corbishley on butterflies, Mattingley on Roman coins. It could have been a clever adolescent's collection. It could have been the remains of a scholar's.

Stella pushed the onions into a pan and conveyed it to the calor gas.

'So what happened?' she repeated as Fresh applied a kitchen towel to the hair of his head and beard.

'The water main, which runs north south through the close, broke near the centre of the green. They've been repairing the main up Colgate and they've been altering the pressure all week. The piping's old, circa 1890, and it finally split.'

'But the wireless said finds of great archaeological interest.'

'Did they?' Fresh smiled. He was full of energy. He was practically dancing as he hung up the towel. 'I told them. I told the old dean. I told the new dean. I told the archdeacon. In fact, I told anyone who'd listen and a lot who wouldn't that the Via Tepiduna went east west through the close. If you look at Dunch's plans of the 1922 dig, it's clear that if they'd let him dig up the close—which, of course, they wouldn't—he'd have hit the south gate of the Roman city.'

Stella was only moderately interested in this. She enjoyed the way Fresh told things more than what he actually said. She swung the cauldron of chicken mash from the stove into his hands. Then she took a small bag of pellets and steered him to the door. The lurcher bitch, who had been stretched out beside the black boiler stove, rose, stretched gracefully and followed them out. The hut formed one of three arranged in an open-sided square. In front was a spruce-looking vegetable garden. The hens were lodged behind. The rain had ceased and a yellow gash in the sky on the other side of the railway line indicated the sun had set.

'So what did you tell them?' she pursued.

'I told them,' Fresh resumed, 'that where there's a gate there's life. That stands to reason.' Just occasionally the local accent with its glottal stop in place of the final 't' could be heard in Fresh's speech. 'It's worth digging at a gate. Trade goes on. Stuff passes. Things'll have come off the back of carts just as they come off the backs of lorries nowadays.'

Fresh distributed the mash evenly along the wooden feeders which he'd made with timber recovered from the river. He was rewarded with a dozen Moran hens falling to with appreciation. The lurcher, who had been left outside the wire run, drooled.

'So why couldn't they let you dig?' Stella broadcast the pellets over the ground.

Some of the Morans found themselves in a dilemma.

'Partly, it's that they're frightened of what they might find. There's a great pile of bones and rams' skulls scattered all round. That's more than they can take, death. They don't want to be reminded. Also,' Fresh dumped the last of the mash and swung the pail round in his hand, 'they don't like me because I'm not pukka. I haven't a university chair in archaeology. You know what the new dean called me? An autodidact.' He flung back his head and laughed in huge pleasure. 'Autos, self, didasko, I teach. He thought it an insult that I'm self-taught. When you think of the archaeologists who've taught themselves. Schliemann, Evans, Ventris. Why, it's a compliment.'

'What was the new dean doing?'

'Trying to get rid of me. He's got silly plans for the west door involving glass, engraved, I shouldn't wonder, with a design of angels. I was trying to dissuade him.'

'But what did you find? Anything?'

They stood together surveying the gobbling fowls.

'They haven't a clue what they've got. Not a clue.'

'Well, what have they got?'

'I told you. A pile of bones and rams' skulls and a Janus.'

'A what?'

'Roman god of gateways. Gates are holy places. Beginnings and ends. Alphas and Omegas. Potent. You need to pray for a safe journey at the start and give thanks for a safe return. Don't you?' He turned to look at her.

'Oh, yes,' said Stella quickly. 'Journeys are dangerous.' She had cause to know.

'They look both ways. Januses.'

'What?'

'The head has two faces back to back.' He swung himself back to back with her.

'Oh,' she said. 'Oh.' Her imagination caught his delight. 'Outwards and inwards.'

'Exactly.'

'And what will happen to it, him? Can we see him?'

'We shored him upright on some scaffold planks, Jack McGrath from the fire brigade and me. It looks,' he paused, 'marvellous. He's well nigh perfect. He looks,' he smiled down at her and fingered his curly beard, 'like me.'

CHAPTER FOUR

SHROVE TUESDAY

Theodora awoke in the clerical bed in her clerical flat and remembered where she was. Her eye followed the flock wallpaper upwards and met the picture rail. Not many of those about nowadays, she thought happily. She had begun to be extremely fond of the flat. She was cheered by the solidity of mahogany, turkey carpets, chairs so heavy that you hurt yourself if you bumped into them and a table which was rock solid. The bed was long enough to sustain her six foot one and broad enough for her arms not to reach the edges if she stretched out.

The place was full of unexpected luxuries. The living room had an open fire place. She had returned about seven the previous evening, cold and sodden from the events in the close and a brief foray round a supermarket and found it laid with wood and coal. Her lunchtime plate and cup had been washed up and put away. There was fresh milk in the fridge and a bottle of sherry on the sideboard. The bedroom window was open three inches and the bed had been turned down. She was at a loss to know to whom she owed these courteous attentions but determined to enjoy them. On the mantel shelf, she found an invitation to the dean's Shrove Tuesday party in the Deanery the following evening. She lit the fire, used a pair of bellows for the first time in her life, poured the sherry and rang Geoffrey.

'What's it like?' he'd inquired, genuinely solicitous.

'Full of incident.' She'd filled him in.

'You sound happy,' he'd said. Was it surprise or resentment, she wondered.

'Well, the Janus is rather jolly. And my boss is the first female residentiary canon in England and she looks engagingly mad.'

'So I've heard.'

'You didn't tell me.'

'Didn't want to raise your hopes. What's your new dean like?'

'I've only heard him bullying an autodidact so far. We haven't been introduced.'

'Who was the autodidact?'

'The archaeologist who dusted off the Janus. Old scores, I should think. Also, there's some sort of feuding going on with the local press who don't like the church or anyway cathedral clergy. I haven't quite worked it out yet.'

'Well, I'm glad it all sounds so promising.' No mistaking the warmth of tone this time. 'I've got adult confirmation at the door. I must rush. Keep me in the picture. Bye then.'

'Bye.'

She had grilled her lamb chops, tossed broad beans from colander to plate, propped open Pedersen's *Israel*, the chapter on 'The sacrifice and its effects' and surrendered to the sheer bliss of solitude and an early night.

Now, the following morning, she stretched luxuriously. Light strengthened and the room began to take shape. The ancient central heating gurgled like some accommodating digestive system. She reviewed with pleasure the day before her. Eight o'clock Eucharist in the cathedral, then a round of visiting names in adult education with Canon Millhaven. In the evening the dean's Shrove Tuesday party. The cathedral bell struck seven. Time to get underway.

Outside in the close, the air was cold but dry, the clouds high. It was possible to feel if not quite spring at least the lessening of winter. The crater had been cordoned off with soft red ropes, presumably snatched in haste from the cathedral. It made a royal enclosure for the object. The Janus on its scaffold planks was suspended over the abyss from which it had risen. It was about four foot tall in black bronze. The body was roughly worked. It was not so much that the arms were missing as that they did not appear ever to have existed. It was nothing more than a head and torso. That head was, however, magnificent. It was enormous and, of course, two-faced. One face looked towards the cathedral, the other towards the city and the fens beyond. The hair and curling beard were styled in rope-like clusters. The mouths were slightly open and the lips were full and prominent. Its eyes were large and staring with, Theodora bent closer, holes where the pupils would be. The face was human in feature, to be sure, but its expression suggested a traveller from another world. The god had the air of surveying and possessing his surroundings.

'It's quite big, isn't it?' said a voice at Theodora's elbow. She looked down and recognised the boy she had pulled from the hole yesterday. 'It's rather,' he sought for his word, 'strong,' he completed.

'Formidable?' Theodora offered.

'Yes. The dean doesn't like it. Nor does the daddy. He called it a pagan horror.'

'I don't think it's any threat to the dean and chapter,' Theodora said reassuringly.

'Well, it will make a difference, won't it?'

'Difference?'

'It's changed things don't you think? People will see there are alternatives.'

Theodora looked again at the far-seeing face and wondered if this precocious child might not be right. The bell for Eucharist began to toll. Timothy moved off towards the Precentory. Theodora turned in the direction of the cathedral. She could have sworn that there was a faint smell of fried bacon proceeding from the south porch door.

* * *

Later in the morning, things hotted up round the cathedral. The world caught on to the fact that there was some new thing to run after. There was a steady stream of people tramping through the close to stop and stare up at the new god. The media hastened to satisfy those who could not come in person.

'I can't tell you any more.' Mrs Perfect looked helplessly into the phone. 'I only know it was a Janus.'

'Yes. I got that,' said the voice at the other end soothingly. 'I've spelt it GENOUS. Right?'

'Wrong,' said Mrs Perfect and set him right. 'Look, I'm sorry I really can't help you any further. We've been told not to say anything to the press or the media.'

The voice expressed incredulity.

'Well, if you want any more information, I suggest you ring the dean on 4673140.' She replaced the receiver before it could make any more demands on her. It wasn't yet ten o'clock and they had already had two nationals on the line, as well as the *Examiner* and Bow Broadcasting. Pagan religion, it seemed, was news.

* * *

The dean clasped the phone rigidly. 'No, I will not be photographed with the Janus. Nor, I think, will the rest of the chapter. You appear to have no understanding of what you are asking and I deeply resent your suggestion that we are, as you put it, all in the same trade. I find your frivolity most offensive.' There was a pause.

'No, I have no desire to be interviewed by you. I may say your paper's last effort at ecclesiastical reporting in the matter of my installation as dean was a totally irresponsible piece of writing. I don't know who does these things for you but you'd do well to sack him. Or her,' he added as an afterthought. The dean had never scrupled to tell other people their business.

He turned back to the memorandum he was composing. 'Dear Bishop,' he wrote, first to the diocesan then to the suffragan. His small neat writing covered the page. The internal post went at 11 a.m. The content was the same as the one he had already penned to the precentor and the archdeacon. Only the tone was different. To Canon Erica Millhaven he hardly thought it worth writing.

* * *

The suffragan bishop in his pleasant house out at Quecourt, a village some ten miles north of Bow, looked at the morning edition of the *Examiner*. The headline ran:

Religious Revival!

> A strange new god has emerged from a pit in the cathedral close. Last night the eminent local archaeologist Oliver Fresh, 44, the Hollow, happened to be present when a water main burst in the cathedral close. Borne on the flood was an object which Mr Fresh rapidly recognised as a statue of the Roman god Janous. The god, who is four foot high and has two heads, has lain asleep

under the cathedral close for sixteen hundred years. He was probably buried when the Romans left the city hurriedly after Rome fell and withdrew her forces from England in AD 400. 'So he's due for a bit of an airing. A resurrection, you might say,' said Mr Fresh last night.

The suffragan did not care for the tone of this. He reached for his pen and began a note to the dean. 'Dear Dean, I wonder if you share my unease at the way in which the media are covering the find of the Janus. While I can fully appreciate the importance for classical studies of a find of this nature, I wonder if the statue is not being used in some subtle way to undermine the Christian faith . . .'

When he had finished with the letter to the dean, he thought of the previous article in the *Examiner*, 'A View from a Pew.' Would they be from the same source, he wondered. The dean, he knew, shared his outrage at it. He'd mentioned it yesterday when they had had their meeting with the archdeacon. The dean had wondered if there was any pressure which could be brought to bear on the paper. The archdeacon had had to explain to the dean that the reason for the *Examiner*'s hostility stemmed from their opposition to the development of the land on which the Hollowmen had settled. Ever since the chapter had applied for planning permission there had been nothing but criticism from the local press. It seemed most unlikely that the editorial policy would be changed to suit the cathedral clergy. A more hopeful approach, the suffragan had suggested, would be to find out who was writing the offending articles and see if they could be dissuaded. The suffragan cast round in his mind for possible allies in the fray. He glanced at his diary. A note in it said, 'Remember T. Braithwaite.' He remembered not Theodora, whom he had not met, but her father whom he had known and trusted. He reflected for a moment. Perhaps the dean's do this evening, which she would surely attend, would provide a suitable opportunity.

* * *

Archdeacon Archibald Gold moved the miniature of the 1925 Silver Ghost from the left-hand side of his desk to the right, ran the end of his gold-plated biro across his teeth twice and finally bent his shoulders almost level with the desk. 'Dear Vince,' he wrote, 'I've got a couple of ideas about our Roman friend. How about an exhibition of cathedral treasures with him as star turn? Or what about starting a permanent heritage centre with him in it? Alternatively we could tour him round. On the other hand we might raise a bit if we sold him off. Either way I think he could be a good little earner for the cathedral in these hard times. Could we discuss?'

* * *

Before eleven o'clock Canon Riddable had written to the Dean. 'Dear Dean, Re Idol: I suggest you get rid of this offensive piece of pagan paraphernalia as soon as maybe. I hardly think I need to point out to a man of your experience the sort of trouble it could cause the chapter. May I draw your attention to Leviticus 19.4.'

* * *

Erica Millhaven swung her VW Golf into a layby without signalling. There was a screech of brakes behind her and an angry flashing of lights before she finally came to rest.

'A word,' she said, turning to Theodora beside her. 'A word in your ear.'

They had spent the day dashing nimbly round the diocese to introduce Theodora to a variety of people concerned with lay education. They had proved to be worthy people of both sexes but mostly advanced in age and comfortable in circumstance. They had greeted Canon Millhaven and herself with great kindness but Theodora found some difficulty in separating them in her mind. She contrasted it with her own parish's ethnic mix where Greeks and Turks, Punjabis and Afro-

Caribbeans jostled the remains of an indigenous London population and the vitality was tremendous.

The relationship with Canon Millhaven had been uneasy. When dealing with business arrangements, comments on courses, suggestions about training, she'd been accurate and efficient. She gave every sign of having hands on ropes. In between meetings, however, as they careered along country lanes, in and out of farmyards and round suburban estates in the uniformly flat countryside, she'd veered from gnomic understatement to expansive intimacy. On one occasion, banking round an acute angle in the road generated by the drainage system of the area, she had exclaimed in answer to Theodora's courteous inquiry about the duties of being a residentiary canon, 'Well, of course chapter are all so idle and so factious, antipathy to my appointment is practically the only thing which unites them and generates any energy.'

So when she turned into the layby and said to Theodora, 'A word,' Theodora did rather wonder to what further indiscretion she might be going to be treated.

'This idol should wake them up,' Canon Millhaven started.

'How?'

'Our society is deeply pagan. People will sympathise with the Janus. He'll become a cult, you'll see.'

'What will they sympathise with?' Theodora was curious. 'I mean, would it rise above the level of adopting a mascot?'

Canon Millhaven gazed through the rain-splashed window. 'We don't seem to know what cathedrals are *for* any more,' she said, apparently at a tangent. 'The chapter, or at least some of them, want to see it as a glorified conference centre. They seem to think it's a place for people to be jolly in. The building itself becomes exhausted by the press of people traipsing through. The new dean wants to tart it up and put gewgaws in. The old dean was past caring. He liked it empty really. He was a man of prayer and he prayed. In his last years I doubt if he noticed anything very much.'

'What *should* the cathedral be for then?'

Canon Millhaven turned with passion towards Theodora. 'Oh, surely you know? A numinous place. A temenos, holy ground, cut off from the world, a meeting of heaven and earth. Quite, quite different from anything round it.'

It had something of that, Theodora thought, recalling the sudden remarkable blotting out of sound which she'd first experienced as her taxi swung under the Archgate and into the close yesterday morning.

'We have to find what our culture most lacks and provide it. We have no business aping the restless world. Those forces of spirituality and piety which have down the ages hallowed and sanctified the place see it now with no more numinosity than an airport.' Canon Millhaven leaned forward across the gear stick and held Theodora's gaze. 'I have spoken,' her tone was hushed, 'with the ancient dead of our cathedral. They are not pleased with us.'

There were few types of eccentricity which Theodora had not met in the course of her ecclesiastical childhood, but, though she'd heard tell of it, this was the first time she had personally encountered talking with the dead. Of course there had been that canon of St Paul's and doubtless others.

'Do you think the Janus might restore the numinous?' Theodora was hesitant.

'In a very low level way,' said Canon Millhaven dismissively. 'The pagan gods are not, of course, important in themselves.' She sounded like an old fashioned landowner describing the tenantry. 'Nevertheless a Janus, looking both ways, is by no means negligible, Miss Braithwaite. Duality,' she exclaimed, 'so important in all the best religions.'

'Inner and outer, dark and light, heaven and earth,' Theodora murmured almost to herself. 'But we can decide though,' she went on more confidently. 'We can choose how to value it, the Janus, I mean, what to let it do to us. Wouldn't you say?'

'We shall need to be very careful, very alert and on our guard,' Canon Millhaven answered briskly. 'Beware in particular, I should say, of the new dean.'

Canon Millhaven sat back in her seat and slipped the car into gear. 'The only truly religious life lived round here,' she said dismissively, 'is down there.' She waved out of the driver's window.

Theodora caught a glimpse, half familiar, of three Nissen huts and some allotments beyond the railway line.

'In the Hollow,' said Canon Millhaven as she hit the main road.

* * *

'Erica Millhaven talks to the dead,' said Theodora when she rang Geoffrey before setting out for the dean's party.

'You don't surprise me,' said Geoffrey. 'I've got adult baptism at the door. I must rush. Keep me in the picture.'

Across the close in the Deanery kitchen, Nick Squires was putting four King's School boys through their paces as waiters before letting them loose on the dean's guests. He'd waited at clergy parties himself when he was their age, two years ago.

'Look, Beddows, you're supposed to be offering it, not trying to hit them with it. They've got a choice, you know. They don't have to eat the stuff.' He took the plate from the grinning Beddows and demonstrated. There was a round of applause.

The kitchen in the basement was large, warm, clean, and stacked with food and drink. All had been beautifully organised by the head verger. The dean had indicated his wishes for this, his first venture into hospitality in his new dignity, and Tristram Knight had seen to it. Nick was much impressed by Tristram. He had style, Nick felt. He watched him and felt more drawn to him the more notice Tristram took of him. He discerned Tristram to be a fixer. He liked his attention to detail, his ability to foresee contingencies, his ease and lack of fuss. In a small way he was imitating him as he ran though the moves again with Beddows and his three happy helpers. A fact which did not escape Tristram as he removed the final corks from the claret.

On the kitchen table was spread the late adition of the *Examiner*. The evening headline ran 'New Gods for Old' and the first sentence, Nick saw, read, 'The dean and chapter of St Aelfric Cathedral are worried about the Janus discovered in the Cathedral close yesterday'.

'The *Examiner*'s running the Janus story for all its worth,' Nick remarked.

Tristram leaned companionably over his shoulder and grinned. 'Not the dean's day,' he said. 'And we haven't finished yet.'

* * *

Upstairs in the entrance hall visitors were

beginning to arrive. It was all suavely organised. Ladies left their coats in the dean's study on the left, the gentlemen pushed on to the cloakroom beyond the staircase. Then they were channelled upstairs to the drawing room on the first floor.

Clerical society is not unlike an archaeological dig. The modern top layer only partly hides much older attitudes and manners. The Church of England is not a *Guardian*-reading democracy of rational equals. It is a hierarchy, and a male hierarchy at that, where the criteria for advancement are decorously unpublished. Promotion, with its overtones of talent and industry, may operate in the secular world; in the clerical, however, it is called preferment and it moves in a mysterious way. 'How on earth did he become ...?' can often only be answered in terms of whom he knows. 'What on earth does he do?' can sometimes not be answered at all.

In such a society wives of clergy have no independent worth and must, therefore, take their rank from their husbands. Accordingly, in the deanery hall, three people hurried to help the diocesan bishops lady off with her serviceable Windsmoor. Those who failed to gain a part in this performance were granted a second chance on the arrival of the suffragan's a few moments later. The two women looked at each other with practised loathing. The suffragan's wife's family had lived in the county for five generations. Her cousinage went in all directions, but mostly up. She never needed to strain. The diocesan's wife had been a nurse before she met the bishop when he had been a curate in Hounslow. Height, a full figure and a large jaw entitled her, she felt, to a leading role, even had Ronald not made the bench. If there were those who did not concur and felt she overestimated her powers, they held their tongues. There was no subject on which she was not willing to give a lead, or, as she put it, set the tone. She was especially inclined to put people right if they were not performing quite as she would wish. God would not mind, Ronald would not notice, but Grace would say a word.

She shook the dean's hand with the air of setting aside rank in favour of Christian brotherhood. 'Well, Vincent, is this a house warming or are you celebrating your find?'

'Find?' The dean stood square and stocky in the middle of the mat in front of his drawing-room hearth, his clerical evening dress immaculate, his little shoes gleaming. He was not a tall man. On a good day he made five foot two. His strong grey hair sprang across his head like Cumberland turf. He gave her a ration of his small smile. 'No find of mine, Grace, I do assure you.' He was noticeably more at ease with his superiors than with his equals or subordinates. Hierarchy breeds such manners.

'Have chapter decided what to do with him?' the bishop asked as he joined his wife. He had taken the precaution of getting a glass in his hand before embarking on the rigours of conversation. He did not need to listen. It was enough for any gathering that he graced it. He allowed his mind to stray to the American holiday for which he was departing early on the morrow.

The dean was saved from having to frame an answer by the arrival of the mayor. 'A sort of secular re-run of the installation,' said the mayor jovially as he pumped the dean's hand up and down. 'Let's hope we're all using the same service sheet, this time.' He laughed affably at the dean who did not respond to his pleasantry.

The room was beginning to fill up. Beside the other fire place, directly opposite the dean and the diocesan bishop, a rival court had gathered round the suffragan and the archdeacon. Various responses to the topic of the moment were being explored.

'The point is, can we make some money out of it?' Archdeacon Gold was saying, swaying to and fro on his jogger's heels. Though perfectly presentably turned out he managed to give the impression he had just come on from Brands Hatch. 'It could be a multi-million pound attraction, if we handled it right.'

Mrs Riddable shivered in a way which

suggested she was demonstrating what shivering was to very young children meeting the concept for the first time. 'It gives me the *creeps*,' she squeaked in her well-known italic delivery. 'All that pagan power, all that concealed *evil* just lying there under the surface waiting, just *waiting* to jump out at us when we weren't expecting it.'

Mrs Riddable's excesses were too well known in her own society to cause comment any more but even the hardened were brought to silence by this. Only the suffragan's wife remained unmoved. She sipped her wine composedly. 'I thought he looked rather a handsome fellow. What do you think, Henry?' she turned to her husband.

'He's beautifully modelled,' Bishop Clement conceded. 'A very high level of craftsmanship. Not, I would have thought, provincial work. Perhaps continental, even Italian.'

Mrs Riddable seemed to think that explained a great deal.

'I do wonder, though,' the suffragan went on, 'whether it isn't rather a pity that he was found so near the cathedral, on consecrated ground. I fear the general public might get the wrong impression.'

'What impression?' said Canon Riddable abruptly, joining the conversation for the first time. 'It's a bit of tin. St Paul tells us what to think about pagan idols. Romans 8.17.'

'Yes, I've read Romans,' said Bishop

Clement mildly, 'but people get attached to things. He may attract the wrong sort of notice.'

'Provided they pay to notice him.' The archdeacon showed his own attachments. 'Then it could be a multi-million pound . . .' He felt an almost physical release as he said this. When he'd been a bank clerk before his conversion, he'd never dreamed he might be able to say things like this and mean them. But the church had given him that opportunity. He was a humble man at heart. He was grateful.

Canon Riddable swung round on the archdeacon whom he overtopped by more than a head. He seemed to threaten him almost physically.

'Historically that idol has no part in our Christian tradition. If we meddle with it, we're damned.'

'We shouldn't be railroaded by tradition,' the archdeacon protested incoherently, taking a step back.

In the doorway of the drawing room Theodora paused. Her height gave her some advantage in gatherings of this kind. She surveyed the scene and saw an eighteenth-century double cube room panelled in white painted wood with rather too little furniture and rather too many people.

Over on the far side of the room she caught the suffragan's eye. She was surprised when he detached himself from his group and made his way across to her.

'Miss Braithwaite? I think we met on the stairs yesterday.'

Theodora smiled her remembrance and gratitude.

'I believe Canon Millhaven may be delayed. I wondered if I might have a word with you a little later on. I have a small commission which you might be able to help us with. I knew your father, of course.' he smiled as though this explained all. 'Now, will you allow me to introduce the dean to you.'

Theodora admired the way he had put this.

'Braithwaite?' said the dean.

Theodora was aware of the double take, the adoption of an attitude and the almost simultaneous revision of it.

'Braithwaite? Are you by any chance related to Nicholas Braithwaite?'

Theodora nodded. 'He was my father.'

'And Canon Hugh?' the dean pursued, anxious not to make a mistake about anything.

'My great uncle,' she conceded.

'I'm delighted to make your acquaintance,' said the dean warmly. Whatever he felt about women, and women in deacon's orders, had to be balanced against the known saintliness of the father and scholarly distinction of the great uncle.

Theodora murmured polite sentiments about being delighted to be in Bow, opportunities to learn, a part of the country unknown to her. Then, as others lined up to claim their host's attention, she was free once more to wander.

Her clerically practised eye took in the groups. The high churchmen of the catholic wing were nearest to her, their hands confidently cradling full glasses. The lowchurchmen, the evangelical tendency, had gravitated to the other end of the room. They mostly solaced themselves with fruit juice. The distinction between these two groups had a sartorial dimension: the clerical collars of the evangelicals were broad, those on the Catholic wing narrow. The higher the collar, her uncle Hugh would have remarked, the lower the churchmanship, In between these two groups were the broad churchmen and the laity. The two knots of the latter Theodora mentally labelled town and gown. Securing a glass from a passing Kingsman she began her perambulations down the room.

'It's certainly beginning to change,' a vigorous-looking young priest was saying. 'We haven't quite reached the stage of Benediction yet, but at the Eucharist I was at last week there were altar boys running around like rabbits,'

'I understand the new dean is sworn to restore proper Catholic worship to the cathedral.'

'What do chapter think of that?' a third member of the group inquired with interest.

'In general, they're against anything which

lengthens the services.'

'How do they plan to stymie him?'

'By a masterful campaign of inactivity. Canon Riddable is a world champion in the art.'

Theodora moved down the room. The broad churchmen were keeping to personalities and politics. Old scores were being paid off, new ones totted up. Archdeacon Gold's tastes in dress, cars and churchmanship did not command the approval of all his colleagues. He had been in the post for three years but he was not a Bow man born and bred. He'd come from some suburban diocese in the south of England. He was fair game, it was reckoned.

'He's scarcely presentable, the archdeacon, would you say?' A silver-haired gentle old man with a concave, ascetic face inquired of a squarer and younger version.

'In what way?'

'Thick?' suggested the concave one tentatively.

'A bit out of his class, certainly,' the other conceded.

'Doesn't know which way's up, would you say, Noel,' he drew in the third member. 'All those real estate deals.' He chewed the Americanism with delight.

'A very different class of shark to the ones he's been used to,' agreed his companion.

'Essentially a man of the sixties,' the silvery

haired one went on, clearly eager to finish the job once he'd started it.

'You mean?'

'Goodwill, of course.'

'Of course.'

'A deep personal commitment.'

'Naturally.'

'But viring a lumpy budget.'

'I see what you mean.'

'Keeping an eye on the small print.'

'Hardly.'

'Putting the right sweeteners round the Borough planning office for the Hollow development.'

'No way.'

'Won't last long with the new dean, would you say?' He slammed the trap shut.

It was all very familiar stuff to Theodora. She skirted the first group of laity which she had labelled town. It consisted of the mayor and a posse of expensively suited local politicians supported by their women folk, all of whom looked as though they might originally have worked for their livings and could again if the need arose. There was a smell of aftershave and many, by the look of their tans, seemed to have recently returned from skiing holidays. The talk was of prices, shares and fat stock.

Beyond them a second group of laity had congregated. These were the ones Theodora had thought of as gown. They were less well turned out than their neighbours but had the air of not caring, of minds on higher things. Their wives wore no make up and were clad in interesting combinations of colours and fabrics. They were dominated by a small broad-shouldered old man whose copious white hair might have been cut at home rather than in a barber's. His small eyes popped beneath bristling white brows. He was smoking triangular Egyptian cigarettes and his high cultivated voice was easily discernible above the babble of others.

'My father, God bless him, always said there was more to come out of the close. There were rams,' skulls, you know, all over the shop. Rams,' he paused and sucked his lips appreciatively, 'were the sacrificial animals of the Janus. Amongst others,' he added.

For a moment it looked as though someone else might get their hands on the conversation, so he pressed uninterruptibly on. 'Though, of course, for the ancients, there was a right and a wrong way to go through a gate, especially to war.' His manner was midway between an old-fashioned WEA lecturer and a military man going over his last campaign. He lacked, Theodora thought, only the epidiascope and pointer.

'What is it Livy says?' he went on. '"*Infelice via*", by an ill-omened path.' The old man's lips split open to reveal appalling teeth. 'Serve the clergy right to have had their old rival lodged in their cellars for fifteen hundred years.

'It's an eerie thought,' said one of the women in attendance. 'Do you suppose it's had an influence? Been at work, as it were?'

'Well, it's had a dramatic enough resurrection, rising out of the abyss on a flood,' said her companion with relish.

'It'll cause a great deal of trouble,' the old man went on. 'Mark my words. Problem one, who owns it? Problem two, what to do with it?'

Theodora edged her way through the crowds. If 'father' was the original archaeologist, would this make the little white-haired gnome his son, Sir somebody Dunch, she wondered. She moved within listening distance of the suffragan's group. Conversation had grown desultory, as of people who had been too long in each other's company.

'Trevor used to play the guitar quite a lot,' Mrs Riddable was saying to the suffragan's wife.

'I somehow thought he might have done,' returned the latter in a neutral tone.

'Can we make some money out of it?' the archdeacon was asking a newcomer to the group.

'Archdeacons only think about money,' murmured a youngish-looking cleric. No one took the least notice of his remark which suggested to Theodora that he might be the succentor. Reckoning she'd had her money's worth conversationally, she turned away.

'A celebration of shared values, Miss Braithwaite.'

Theodora looked at the tray-carrying figure who had addressed her. She had a flash of memory. 'Did I see you verging at the eight o'clock this morning?' she inquired.

'Quite so. I have the honour to be the dean's verger as well as his head waiter for this evening. My name, by the way, is Tristram Knight.'

'How do you do,' murmured Theodora. She was a bit overwhelmed by the man's presence, his theatricality, his air of addressing an audience wider than herself. He was as tall as she, pale and thin to the point of emaciation. His head was set on his neck in such a way as to appear to slope back from his chin. The black jacket, Theodora judged, was not hired. The shirt, if she were not mistaken, was linen. There was a sort of muted foppishness about him. His voice was educated. He might not be what he appeared to be.

'I thought I would take this opportunity of introducing myself because my young colleague, Nick Squires,' Tristram jerked his head in the direction of the far end of the room, 'is looking after your lodgings. Please don't hesitate to let him or me know if there's anything you want done. Nick's a willing lad.'

Theodora felt it was better not to take up the theme he offered. Instead she tried, 'Does the dean entertain a lot?'

'The last dean was known for his thrift. The size of his sherry glasses was remarked amongst the chapter to be the smallest compatible with hospitality. On the other hand he was eighty when he retired last year. So he had the excuse of age. It is said that in his youth he had laid down a modest cellar and when that ran out in his seventy-fifth year he saw no point in reordering.'

'You've had a long interregnum?' Theodora inquired.

'Six months officially. But the new dean has been at work here for the past month before his installation.'

'Have you been here long?' Theodora thought it safe to inquire.

'Long enough, I'm beginning to feel.' And with that he manoeuvred his tray over the heads of two passing clergy and disappeared.

The dialogue confirmed Theodora's sense of unease. She was aware of an edginess in the gathering, an undertow of disquiet amongst the guests. Was it the advent of a new dean amongst entrenched clergy? Was it the time of the ecclesiastical year, with Lent starting tomorrow? Or was it the Janus? Of course a new dean would be a difficulty for the chapter. Two of them, the archdeacon and the precentor were of a different churchmanship from the dean. He, like the suffragan, was from the Catholic, they from the evangelical wing.

There would be tensions in how worship was ordered, how the furnishing and fabric of the building were treated, how, if one were honest the Christian gospel was interpreted and recommended to the world. Moreover, how things were done in the cathedral would influence and set an example to the rest of the diocese. But all that was par for the course. Every diocese all the time. She sensed something more difficult to define, some tension more cryptic than mere differences in churchmanship. Theodora was surprised to find how many people were stirred by the finding of the Janus.

The fight between the Christian god and the pagan ones had taken place two thousand years ago. The pagan had lost, or anyway gone underground, throughout Europe and in Britain. Surely warfare was not going to be joined again? Why was that bronze figure so threatening? It was alien, of course, like a visitor from an antique land. Its solid presence had authority and the strangeness of its head facing two ways intrigued and challenged. She could understand that the commonplace clergy might feel uneasy. A god of beginnings was also a god of returns. She felt irrationally that it had come back to settle some ancient score.

There was a crash at the far end of the room near the dean followed by a babble of voices and a shriek. One of the King's school waiters could be seen blushing in a litter of broken glass. One of the politicians' wives was brushing claret from her dress and fending off the fuss of others.

'There,' said Mrs Riddable in triumph, 'I told you so. The *evil* works.'

'Pandemonium,' exclaimed the concave priest with relish.

The hubbub died down. The dean led the way into the supper room. The smell of roast pigeon invited.

Theodora found herself involved in the suffragan's party. As they processed towards the dining room, Bishop Clement turned his charming smile upon her and drew her aside, out of hearing of the rest of the crowd.

'I very much admired your article in this quarter's *CHR* on Thomas Henry Newcome,' he began. 'It was a fine piece of detection to recover the material for the missing years 1874–6.'

Theodora was surprised and (what author is not?) gratified by this praise of her first modest venture into academic publishing. 'I enjoyed doing it. And of course there is an archive at St Sylvester's House which is next door to the parish church where I'm currently curate.'

'Ah yes.' The bishop was courteous but clearly biding his time to pursue his own interests. 'I tend to forget Newcome founded two houses, a London one as well as the Yorkshire one. I've heard remarkably good things of the work done there.'

Theodora was immensely pleased. The tractarian priest, the Reverend Thomas Henry Newcome had founded his order, the Society of St Sylvester, in the late nineteenth century. It had followed a Catholic rule and trained priests for urban parishes. Latterly the London house had undergone something of a resurgence; it was known for its treatment of mental illness. She had spent some late nights going through the archive material as a way of keeping alive interests which the pastoral work of the parish might otherwise have driven away. She had read the letters, sermons, diaries and monographs which Newcome had left behind and become increasingly drawn to a character at once complex and naive, self-deluding and principled. She'd thought of doing a life of him and approached Ivan Markewicz, a friend from Oxford days and now editor of *Church History Review,* to test the water. He'd advised trying an article first and been flatteringly pleased with the result.

'You obviously know your way about the world of journalism,' said the bishop firmly recalling her to his own wishes.

Theodora was amused that he classified *CHR* as lightweight, journalism. It wasn't in the front rank of international scholarship, but it was respectable enough to be found in most university libraries. I wouldn't say that. I did my bit at Oxford and took my turn in editing cathedral newsletters in Nairobi. But it wouldn't get me a job on the *Independent.*' She wondered where on earth the bishop was heading.

The bishop revealed his hand. 'We've been having rather a rough ride at present with our local press.'

'So I've noticed.' Theodora thought it as well not to smile.

'Ah, you've read the *Bow Examiner* on the dean's installation perhaps?'

Theodora nodded. 'Such hostility to the church in a small community is unusual surely?'

The bishop had obviously anticipated that reaction. He outlined the cause of the hostility and the feeling about the redevelopment of the Hollow. 'Tempers often run high in money matters,' he said forgivingly and, as Theodora knew, from the safety of a private income. 'There's no doubt that the cathedral's finances would benefit from a sale of the land down at the Hollow. Nor can we continue our ministry in this world without the wherewithal. Of course the *Examiner* has a right to put its point but this vilification of the cathedral's rituals is no proper way to pursue the matter.' He swung round to face Theodora. 'Wouldn't you agree?'

Theodora met his eye with her own level gaze. She weighed the fact that she did not agree with him against the fact that he was a bishop and she in deacon's orders.

'The author of "A View from a Pew" seemed

to feel that the cathedral's ministry had fallen below an acceptable standard in fairly straightforward ways,' she said. 'It failed, in his opinion, to generate an atmosphere of prayer and seemed to celebrate the worldly and political aspects of the appointment.'

She'd compromised. She'd said what she thought but in a tone so gentle that she might have been agreeing with him. It was a measure of his quality that he listened to both words and tone. He paused. Then he replied almost curtly. 'If the author has serious points to make he should have signed it with his own name.'

Theodora was so much in agreement with this that she was caught off guard by his next move.

'I think it would help both the author himself as well as us to know who it is. I wondered if you would feel able to exercise your talent for detection in doing that.' The bishop had reached his point.

'Me?' Theodora was astonished.

'With your journalistic experience,' the charming smile had returned. 'For the good of the church and of course the writer,' he concluded.

This was preposterous. This gentle, courteous man wanted to prevent free speech and cared more about the appearance of the church in the world than its spiritual reality.

'You will help us, will you not, Miss Braithwaite?'

They are none of them above image-making, Theodora thought with sudden disgust. Then she remembered his kindness in taking her under his wing and introducing her to the dean. She intuited, too, his real gentleness in human relationships. It was just possible that he saw a pastoral need to minister to anyone who could write as bitterly as the author of 'A View from a Pew'. 'Why not ask the editor who writes these pieces?' It was a forlorn hope she knew.

'That has of course been tried. He won't divulge his source. What we need is a discreet piece of private inquiry. For the church.'

He knew he had got her. She had eight generations of Anglican clerical ancestors who had all, more or less, done what their bishops had required of them. 'I suppose I could ask around a bit.' She knew she sounded ungracious.

The bishop absolved her of any lack of grace. He shone the light of his smile upon her. 'Splendid. I knew I could rely on you. Your father was such a dear man. Supper,' he said hungrily and led the way forward.

No further untoward incident occurred. At a quarter before midnight the party broke up. Many clergy would have early ashes services at which to officiate on the morrow, Ash Wednesday. The diocesan bishop and his wife had to catch an early plane to America. Theodora retrieved her coat from the dean's study and joined the guests trooping out into the bitter March night. In the middle of the close could be seen the mound of earth marking the archaeological activities of the earlier part of the day. Someone had draped the Janus in black polythene which the gusty wind had partially removed. It flapped suddenly and loudly as though indecorously, importunately demanding their attention. The cathedral clock chimed midnight.

CHAPTER FIVE

DUST AND ASHES

The dean's body was found the following morning, stretched out in front of the Janus. The throat had been cut from ear to ear. Blood had soaked into the damp grass on that side of the statue which faced towards the cathedral. Dennis Noble had found him when he'd crossed the close to ring the bell for the early ashes service.

Dennis had raised the alarm at about seven-thirty a.m. By eight-thirty Inspector Spruce of the Norfolk CID, on loan to the Bow Constabulary for a six-month secondment, had been summoned from his fenland fastness. As he put the telephone down in the farmhouse where he lodged, his spirits leaped up. He had never known such boredom as his four months in Bow had afforded him up to now. As he reached for his Barbour, Spruce had to check himself saying, 'What fun'. Of course murder wasn't fun. It meant a gaping hole in the proper order of things. It meant, usually, someone deranged with fear and danger and getting rid of those unendurable passions in the most complete and primitive way possible. But, God, he'd been bored and now he wasn't. Hume, was it, who said he could wish the whole universe destroyed provided only that the pain in his little finger was healed.

The cathedral was coping. His sergeant had met him at the Archgate with the words, 'They wouldn't cancel their service but I have got them to close the place off now. And I've got them to give us a room next door to their offices. They weren't for that, at first. Needed a bit of persuading. Seemed to think once the body was removed we could operate from the station.'

Spruce nodded. He'd worked amongst the clergy once before. There'd been that priest chap had his neck broken out at St Benet Oldfield last summer. The clergy had been none too helpful on that occasion. He knew the pitfalls.

'Still,' his sergeant pressed on, 'they saw my point when I said we might have to install ourselves in the Deanery.'

Spruce glanced round the close. It was full of strong men with new satchels of expensive camera equipment and very young looking uniformed policemen. Spruce could imagine what a repopulation of the close with these alien bodies would mean to the clergy: a closing of the ranks to resist the invader, no doubt.

'That'll be the Deanery?' he hazarded.

'Right. And over there ...'

'Yes,' said Spruce. 'I see.'

He strode over to the centre of the green sward towards the gash of piled earth and rubble. The grass was spongy from thawed out frost. Spruce ducked under the fluttering white tapes which marked out the dean's resting place. The Janus reared above swathed in polythene and sacking which had been taped over his shoulders like some primitive toga. The dean guarded by the Janus, Spruce reflected.

He drew back the grey blanket covering the body. The mortal remains of Vincent Stream were dressed in clerical evening dress. A black belted gabardene had been flung round the shoulders. The wiry grey hair was splattered with mud and rain. His arms were crossed over his breast in a parody of Christian burial. He looked younger than his probable fifty-odd years. His small assertive face, purged of tension and ambition, had relaxed so that his expression was vulnerable, almost boyish.

Spruce looked down at the corpse's crossed arms and shivered. 'Was he like this when he was found? I mean nobody crossed his arms for him?'

'Nobody's tampered with him. I'm sure. That's how he was.'

'He dressed to come out then.'

'Sir?'

Spruce indicated the stout brown leather walking brogues, heavily caked with mud, which did not match the clerical evening dress. 'What happened?'

'We only know the dean had a party last night at the Deanery to celebrate his promotion. It was Shrove Tuesday. Last day before Lent.'

'Yes, yes,' Spruce said. 'I know the Church's year. So?'

'Well there were about thirty guests. Came about eight and left mostly before midnight.'

'Who?'

'Top town, top clergy. Very select.'

'Got a list?'

The sergeant shook the computerised pages free from his mackintosh pocket.

'Who saw him last?'

'Guests? Canon Riddable, the precentor—he lives over there—may have been the last to leave. Or it might be the head verger, dean's verger he's properly called, a man named . . .' he consulted his list, 'Knight. Tristram Knight.'

'What was he doing at the party?'

'He wasn't. He was serving. Supervising the food and that.'

'Doctor's report?'

'Doctor Gibbon could only spare a moment, he's got a suicide out at Fenny Drain. At the moment he's saying between half twelve and half one last night. Death due to wound in throat. Forensic'll tell us more when he gets him down the morgue.'

Spruce bent and looked again at the body. Gingerly he lifted the left wrist. On it was a plain gold watch on a leather strap. The watchglass had been smashed, caught perhaps on a stone as the dean fell. The hands said ten past one. 'Needn't wait for forensic on that one anyway.'

Spruce glanced at his sergeant. He was a tall thin young man with long black sideburns, a pallid, unhealthy-looking skin and large dark circles under his eyes. His forehead, which was wider than his jaw, shone. His adam's apple bulged. He reminded Spruce of cartoons of Victorian funeral mutes in early numbers of *Punch*. He'd worked with him now for four months and trusted him implicitly for dogged, thorough information gathering of the kind that brighter, pushier young policemen sometimes despised.

'How about weapon?'

'Nothing so far. The wound's very clean; we might be looking for something like an old-fashioned cut-throat razor or a tool, stanley knife, something of that sort.'

'Place, then? He wasn't killed here, was he.'

It was a statement. Spruce looked round measuring the distance of the body from the Deanery, cathedral and offices. It was, like the Janus, equidistant. Spruce indicated the brown brogues on the feet of the corpse. 'The eye holes, the laces are bunged up with mud. He was dragged across soggy earth by the look of it. The question is, which direction was he being dragged from?'

Sergeant Mules pointed towards the cathedral. 'If that's right, it would explain that.' He gestured in the direction of lawn edge outside the south door of the cathedral. Spruce saw what he meant at once. The turf, which had received the attention of gardeners for several centuries, was almost nine inches deep where it met the gravel. At that point the earth had been crumpled and the smart, sharp edge of the lawn was torn away.

'Time one ten a.m. No weapon. Place, probably outside south door of cathedral,' Spruce summarised. 'What about motive?'

The sergeant shook his head. 'It seems inconceivable that a man of the cloth should be done in like this.'

Spruce noticed the old-fashioned phrase, 'man of the cloth'. He knew, however, rather more, he felt, than his sergeant, about the vagaries of the clergy. Of course, it could be some passing maniac. But somehow Spruce rather doubted that. The type of wound and above all the placing, almost the arranging of the body deliberately in front of the Janus, suggested something more complex. He looked up at the bronze figure on its plinth of scaffold board. The dark beard was rimed with white frost. The handsome face stared stolidly over his own head at the cathedral.

You must have seen it all, Spruce found himself thinking. 'Come on,' he said with unwonted curtness to the sergeant. 'Let's see what the cathedral yields.'

* * *

Nick Squires pushed the plate across the vestry table towards Dennis Noble.

'You need sustenance,' he said with solicitude.

Dennis turned his head away from the freshly made bacon sandwich. 'I can't fancy it,' he said. 'It's left me queasy. All those questions the police asked.'

Nick looked at him speculatively. 'What about?'

'About what not,' said Dennis with a sudden turn of angry energy. 'I didn't harm the poor gentleman. I kept telling them I only found him. But when, where, why, how, who, they kept on something rotten.' He sounded near to tears but whether because of the dean's demise or the harassment of the police questioners, Nick could not tell.

'Did they want to know ...?' he began.

'I'd better go and sort them chairs,' Dennis said firmly. Vergers spend much time in moving large number of chairs about Nick reflected. 'And you ought to do something about that sound system. It's got out of hand.' He made it sound like a delinquent child. Morosely he turned to go.

'Poor Dennis,' murmured Nick as he reached for the sandwich before following his colleague.

*   *   *

Theodora raised her eyes from the service sheet and gazed towards the high altar. The frontal was purple for the season of Lent. Strong silvery light entered through the clerestory windows in the choir and glanced off the processional cross propped on the north side of the altar. The ashes service had gone ahead in spite of the dean lying dead in the close. She had watched the head verger, the dean's verger, conduct the suffragan bishop, who was evidently a canon of the cathedral, to his stall. Canon Riddable, the precentor and canon in residence, she remembered from her scanning of the notice in the office waiting room, took the service. His hand trembled and his voice came and went as though it was a wireless with fading batteries. The words of the liturgy echoed in her mind. 'Remember, O man, that thou art dust and to dust thou shalt return.'

Now the small congregation had gone drawing their coats about them as though to protect themselves from some contagion. The cathedral was empty and silent. Canon Millhaven's words of yesterday came back to her. 'It should be quite different from anything else round it. A place where heaven and earth meet. Numinous.' Well, so it was, Theodora thought, in spite of the best efforts of Victorian chapters and philistine deans. In a way the building well represented the city in which it was placed. Bow St Aelfric was plastic and composite to its fingertips. Car parks, roundabouts, leisure centres and shopping malls had replaced all but a few of the earlier buildings, obliterating for the most part the more measured and wholesome life of previous centuries. Just every now and again the unwary tourist or the indigenous inhabitant might bark his shins on the real, that stratum of earth and water which underlay the contemporary clutter. At night or in fog or snow, the older realities asserted themselves. They signalled their presence by a change in temperature, a smell or a quality of silence as now and in this place.

The Janus, rearing itself up from the abyss, Theodora thought, was a reminder of what has been overlaid by tarmac. What would the cathedral do with that reality now confronting it? And what would the clergy make of their horror, the murder of their dean?

She thought again of the small crumpled heap at the foot of the statue, its throat cut like a sacrificial animal. She turned back to the collect for Ash Wednesday. 'Almighty God, who hatest nothing that thou hast made.' Well someone had hated the dean enough to kill him. Whose job would it be to find out who? Would the murderer have been at the party? Was it a man or a woman, clergy or laity? And why? What, in the life and conduct of Vincent Stream, had brought him to this unseemly end at the moment of his triumph? She made her last prayer, 'for the soul of thy servant, Vincent, that he may rest in peace and light perpetual shine upon him.'

'Ah,' said Inspector Spruce to Theodora as she came down the shallow steps of the south porch of the cathedral, 'I thought it must be you.'

Theodora focused her gaze on the neat, gymnastic figure of the inspector with genuine pleasure. At least if there was murder in the cathedral, Spruce she knew was about as good as could be hoped for to solve it. He brought back the memory of a holiday in Norfolk and another clerical death. It had been the first time she had known a policeman, as she put it to herself, in detail. She had been cheered by Spruce's alert and sympathetic intelligence.

'I had no idea,' Theodora began. 'Surely this is outside your usual beat?'

'I'm here on secondment from Norwich,'

Spruce explained. 'Six months. And you? Are you part of the cathedral establishment?'

'Like you, I'm being trained.'

'When I saw the list,' Spruce was pressing on, 'I thought there couldn't be more than one Reverend Braithwaite.'

'Actually,' said Theodora with dignity, 'there are seven Braithwaites currently in orders and I am related to five of them.'

'Visiting are you?' Spruce was not abashed.

'My archdeacon feels I need stretching. I am learning how to educate the laity.'

'How very interesting,' Spruce murmured. Theodora liked him because it was impossible to tell from his tone whether he was being ironical or not.

'Been here long?'

It was instantly clear to Theodora where Spruce was heading.

'I've been here a mere forty-eight hours and I scarcely know my way round the close, never mind the *dramatis personae*. 'And then to make it quite clear she added, 'I am not a sleuth. Last time was an accident. The bishop got hold of me. I couldn't refuse.' She was aware of a note of desperation in her tone which she sought to exorcise.

'Of course. Of course,' Spruce soothed. 'All the same, the clergy are going to need,' he chose his term, 'handling. Specialist knowledge.'

'Snoop on one's own colleagues?' Theodora

said with distaste.

'No, no,' Spruce took himself in hand, realising he wasn't advancing down the right path. He halted suddenly and swivelled on his heel to face the cathedral. Theodora turned with him.

'Nothing like this,' he gestured towards the building, 'can function properly with something like this,' he jerked his head back towards the Janus and its body. 'Whatever places like this are for, whatever good they can bring about, will be vitiated as long as there is a murderer undetected and unpunished in its midst.'

'Yes,' said Theodora. 'Yes, of course. You're absolutely right.'

Spruce relaxed. He did not say, did not need to say (but Theodora quite understood him to mean) that keeping one's hands unsullied and behaving with clerical decorum wasn't going to solve this one. And she quite saw that without allies things would be difficult for Spruce. The clergy, she reflected, were past masters at obstruction and evasion.

'Pooling resources,' Spruce pressed his advantage home, 'complementary techniques formal and informal, might speed things up. Yes? What I mean is, you move more easily amongst these people,' he gestured round the close, 'than any policeman could hope to. You'll hear things and they'll talk to you in ways they certainly aren't going to talk to me or my men. And then there are the children, Riddable's kids, I can't question them officially without a parent and a WPC present. I ask you, what am I going to learn in that sort of set-up?'

'Yes,' said Theodora. 'Yes, of course. I see all that but …'

'But what?'

'Haven't you neglected the fact that I too must be on your list of suspects?'

'Of course.' Spruce was in no way shocked or rejecting of this fact. 'What I feel is that, if I trust you, the gain outweighs the loss. What I need to do above all else is to get some smell of a motive. This is an elaborate, planned crime. It doesn't look like an impulse killing. Someone wanted Dean Stream dead. Now why? Why should a blameless man of the cloth evoke such hatred that someone went to the trouble not just of killing him but of then dragging the body to the foot of the Janus and laying him out with his arms crossed? I need to know as much as possible about Stream and his colleagues. The faster I can do that the better and I hope I've convinced you that someone of your particular background would be invaluable. That doesn't mean to say that I shan't put you on my list of suspects.'

Spruce smiled. But it was because Theodora knew he meant what he said that she replied, 'All right. All right then. I'll do what I can in that one area of research into motives.'

‘Spot on,’ said Spruce with satisfaction.

‘Breakfast,’ said Theodora. She had been to early service fasting. The cold morning was beginning to get to her.

‘Come and have a bite in my flat. I’m next door to the cathedral offices. By the look of it it’s also over the top of your incident room. Very symbolic.’

Spruce kindled the fire and made coffee and toast. Theodora grilled bacon and scrambled eggs. Afterwards Spruce spread out Sergeant Mules’ guest list on the table and added his own and Doctor Gibbon’s preliminary report.

‘Time of death 1.10 a.m. Death due to a single blow to the throat. The wound runs from left to right. Suggests a right-handed assailant. Weapon for the throat wound probably stanley knife, razor or similar thin-bladed instrument.’

Theodora swallowed hard.

‘I’m sorry,’ said Spruce. ‘I’m not sure how much you really need to know the detail of all this.’

‘I suppose it’s as well to know the worst.’ Theodora steeled herself. ‘I saw some horrifying wounds when I was in Africa. And my present parish in south London has its bloody affrays. It’s just that somehow I never quite get used to what man can do to man.’

‘It could be woman,’ he said. ‘That is, if we’re keeping an open mind.’ He ran his index finger down the list. ‘Do I gather that Canon

Millhaven is a member of the cathedral chapter?'

'Yes. She's the most junior member. They haven't allowed women in deacon's orders to hold residentiary canonries for very long. But she's fairly senior in the diocese. She's got rooms in the close over the Archgate. What makes you say it could be a woman?'

'Canon Millhaven is a tall woman, I gather. Dean Stream was a small man.'

'I'd point out that I am a tall woman.' Theodora's six foot one communicated itself through her voice.

'I'm not forgetting that,' said Spruce equably. 'We agreed, didn't we? Now then, was she at the dean's party last night?'

'If she was I certainly didn't see her. I seem to recall the suffragan saying something about her being delayed. Have you a guest list?'

'Yes, we got one off the dean's verger.'

'Tristram Knight?'

'Right. Do you know him or either of the other two vergers?'

'Hardly at all. The younger one, Nick Squires, seems to make himself useful round the close in a number of capacities. For example he services my rooms, at Canon Millhaven's request. The oldest one I've only seen at work heaving chairs about. The senior one, dean's verger, Tristram Knight I think may not be what he seems.' Theodora told him of their conversation at the party. 'The only other thing I know about them is they cook bacon sandwiches in the vestry.'

Spruce looked impressed. 'Not bad for someone who knows nothing of the close and has only been here forty-eight hours. We'll be having a go at all three of course. In fact I think Mules has started on the old man because he found the body. But could you do a bit about either of the others?'

'I could probably do the youngest. He ought to be thanked for buttling round my rooms.'

'And the Riddable children?'

'I could probably do something there too. Mrs Riddable has kindly asked me for coffee this morning.'

'Splendid.' Spruce happily ticked a number of names and columns on his list. 'How about motive? I imagine cathedrals have their own tensions. Have you picked up anything which might give a reason for murder?'

Theodora thought of the dean's party and its undertow of unease. It wasn't enough to put forward at this moment. 'There's some sort of feuding going on between the cathedral chapter and the local press,' she offered and recounted her conversation with Bishop Clement at the party.

Spruce was amused. 'So the bishop enlisted you as a sleuth before ever I got to you.'

'You could put it like that,' Theodora's tone was frosty.

'Could it have anything to do with the

murder do you suppose?'

'I don't know. The tone of the articles was vitriolic. Someone clearly feels that chapter is incompetent at a fairly basic level, the level of celebrating the liturgy. And Bishop Clement feels that tempers are running high about the cathedral's need for money and their method of getting it by selling off the land at the Hollow. There might be something there.'

'Since the bishop's commissioned you,' Spruce saw no reason not to rub it in, 'May I leave you to see if you can turn up anything else in that line? Of course I'll keep it in mind when I question the rest of the list.'

Theodora nodded unhappily.

Spruce ticked some more of his list and after a moment raised his head. 'I suppose the Roman chap in the quad couldn't be a motive for murder?' His tone was almost apologetic. Other policemen would have ridiculed him he knew. But Theodora appeared not to find the question silly.

'It's certainly disquieted the chapter. They seem almost to fear him. But I don't know how that would translate into a motive for murder.'

Spruce did not pursue the topic. Instead he leaned forward and, as though offering the menu at a good restaurant, inquired. 'What about the chapter? What have you got for me there?'

'What do you want?'

'I wouldn't mind knowing what a chapter *is*

for a start and what it does.'

'I'll have to give it some thought,' said Theodora.

CHAPTER SIX

CLERICAL OPINIONS

'Do you read your stars, Miss Braithwaite?'

Rebecca Riddable smoothed out the *Bow Examiner* on the table in the Precentory kitchen. Theodora looked from face to face of the young Riddables. Rebecca was a thin child of about twelve with long straight mousy hair and a look of her mother. Her youngest brother of about seven was fair-haired and bullet-headed, his pale eyes had a look of anxiety which later he might learn to commute into anger and thus resemble his father. Timothy, the middle child, was a square and solid ten year old who resembled neither his brother nor his sister. He'd found the Janus, albeit inadvertently, been interviewed by the press and coped with it all with composure. Their heads, at Theodora's entry, had been clustered together as they pored over the astrological chart. Theodora thought of replying that you couldn't both believe in an almighty and generous God and also think that the stars determine your lives.

'I'm Leo,' she said equably, instead.

'So am I,' said Timothy.

Rebecca knew her hostessly duties. 'I'm Pisces, Ben's Cancer,' she said as though making introductions.

'What is it you want to know from the stars?' asked Theodora, impelled by curiosity.

'I want to know what's going to happen,' said Ben.

'I want to know what I'm like,' said Rebecca.

'But surely someone else can't *tell* you what you're like, you know yourself, and you surely want to *choose* what you're going to become, not have it all laid out for you.' Theodora was reasonable rather than religious.

There was a silence. 'What if you can't?' said Rebecca, her voice a wail, 'What if it's all laid down for you before you were born?'

'Why should it be? How do you know it is?'

'It sometimes feels like that. No one would choose to be born Clergy, into a family like ours, I mean.'

Theodora caught a glimpse of the problem. 'I was,' she said.

'And was that what you wanted?'

'I wouldn't have had it any other way. It was an immense blessing, a privilege.' Theodora realised she'd been drawn into more than she normally allowed.

'Well,' said Timothy firmly, 'there are too many things you can't do if your father's a clergyman. And I want to keep rabbits.'

Theodora didn't quite see the connexion.

'If you live in a close, you mustn't annoy the other chapter members.'

'And rabbits would?' Theodora was curious.

'I think rabbits should be free range and I can see it might be difficult in the close but I can't see what harm a tortoise would do. They're very unobtrusive.'

'You can always go and see the rabbits at the Hollow,' said Ben. 'They run about everywhere there.'

'Daddy doesn't like us to go to the Hollow. He says they're all new agers and perverts.'

The kitchen was large and warm. A cauldron of washing boiling on the large old gas stove threw off clouds of steam. The grey walls were running with condensation. Theodora had tried the front door and got no response. Mrs Riddable had offered coffee at eleven. It was five to. Wise in the ways of clerical families she'd looked around for other methods of entry. The iron staircase had invited to the basement.

'The Janus has two faces,' said Timothy suddenly. 'Does that mean choice?'

'Look both ways,' said Rebecca who had to see the other two across the road.

'Daddy doesn't care for the Janus,' said Ben. 'He says it stands for dark and unloving powers.'

'Mummy says it has claimed its first

sacrifice,' said Timothy.

'The dean shouldn't have been walking about the close late at night near the old god.' Rebecca was nannyish.

'Was the dean out last night?' Theodora prompted.

'Well, I waited up to see Mummy and Daddy home after the party,' Rebecca said. 'Only I fell asleep. When I woke up the clock said a quarter to one and they'd both come in. But I looked out of the window of my room and I saw the dean coming out of the Deanery.'

'Which way was he going?' Theodora inquired.

'He was going to the cathedral.'

'Wasn't it rather late to be doing that?'

Rebecca shrugged. 'It's his cathedral,' she said dismissively. 'Anyway,' she concluded hastily, 'Mummy's in now. I just heard the front door. Would you like to go upstairs. I expect she's expecting you. Ben will show you the way.'

Theodora allowed herself to be ushered out of the kitchen and guided up the basement stairs.

'Daddy didn't like the dean,' said Ben fixing his eyes on hers. Theodora made no comment. It seemed to her that Ben's main social function was to echo his father's condemnatory judgements. Would Ben be destined for the Church, Theodora wondered.

'I couldn't sleep last night,' Ben said lightly

as he shepherded her up the last few stairs to the ground floor. 'I don't think Daddy came back with Mummy. He came back a bit later.' He took his eyes from Theodora's.

'When would that have been?'

'I heard the clock strike one.'

*   *   *

Mrs Riddable unpacked her shopping carriers on the dining-room table. The table was large and filled most of the room. It was not clear to Theodora where she was supposed to station herself in relation to her hostess. She played safe and edged her way round to the empty fireplace. There was no fire but a handful of dusty-looking pine cones with the remains of gilt paint on them failed to decorate the grate. The room was formidably cold. Mrs Riddable took from the top of one of the carriers a large plastic-looking wallet and from the other carrier a large plastic looking purse. These she ranged beside a plastic key case.

'Never put all your eggs in one basket,' she said gaily. 'Now how about coffee. I'm starving. Just ring twice on that bell would you?' She indicated the brass bell-push beside the fireplace and Theodora did as she was told.

Theodora continued to watch fascinated as Mrs Riddable laid out the domestic economy of her family on the dining-room table. The basis was washing powder, three sorts in tremendous quantities. This was supplemented by cornflakes in similar industrial quantities, four packets of fish fingers and three large economy size frozen mixed vegetables. You could chase this down with a large jar of pale, shredless marmalade, six individual fruit pies and an unpleasantly veined chunk of polythene-wrapped Stilton.

'Trevor has an enormous appetite,' said Mrs Riddable as though to deprecate the bounty strewing the table.

Theodora's social nerve was beginning to fail her. She could think of nothing whatever appropriate to say to this.

'Have you lived here long?' she tried desperately.

'It seems an age. In fact it's only five years. We came eighteen months after Ben was born. It was a big sacrifice. It meant Trevor had to give up his research. He was a church historian, you know. He was absolutely *brilliant*, making a *tremendous* name for himself.' The italic delivery was in evidence. 'He's had a couple of things in *Church History Review* and they'd been *terribly* well received. Trevor had some really *appreciative* letters from some of the parish clergy here. And of course his father, poor old fellow, was so proud of him before he died. He'd dabbled a bit in that field himself but hadn't got anywhere. So when Trevor made a success he was over the *moon*. But of course when we came down here, Trevor had to give it all up.' Mrs Riddable dramatised this sacrifice with every inch of her body. 'All of it,' she added, lest Theodora should suppose otherwise. 'Of course you have to take preferment when it's offered.' Mrs Riddable spoke as though it had been offered to both her husband and herself. 'But to be honest I did rather prefer All Saints, Forest Hill. We had some really super folks there. *Terrific* support in the parish. Trevor always said he couldn't manage without them. And some of them had really important jobs. In the City, you know. You know where you are with a parish. I mean, it's all clear about what you're supposed to do.'

Mrs Riddable stopped as though she might have embarked on deep waters.

'I imagine it might be more difficult to find a personal ministry as a wife of a residentiary canon than as the wife of a parish priest.' Theodora was sympathetic.

Mrs Riddable's response to this suggested she was short of understanding listeners. 'That's absolutely *right*. People don't *realise*. It's all right for Trevor. He's, of course, *terrifically* important and very busy as precentor. Up to his eyes. Never has a moment. And of course he was born to it. His father was a canon of Lincoln. But I do sometimes wonder what I'm supposed to do. Though, of course, wife and mother must come first and that takes a lot of time.' Theodora thought of the frozen vegetables and murmured that she was sure it did. At this point the door was flung open and Rebecca appeared with a tray containing two cups of coffee and a jug of cold milk.

'You don't take sugar, do you? Most people don't nowadays,' Mrs Riddable informed her. Theodora, who did if the coffee were powdered, agreed that few people did.

'How are the children coping with the dean's death?' Theodora ventured when they'd addressed the coffee.

Mrs Riddable leaned forward. 'Trevor says it's all the fault of that *idol.* Massive unconscious forces, he says, are at work and the dean should never have come here in the first place.'

'How does he think the idol affected the murder of the dean?' Theodora carefully kept irony out of her tone.

'How can we ordinary mortals tell?' Mrs Riddable was dismissive. 'The fact is that it's been lurking in the grounds of the cathedral for nearly two thousand years waiting to claim its victim. Now it's sprung.'

Theodora hated irrationality or hysteria. She scented both here. 'Surely physical strength rather than numinous power is needed to slit a throat.'

'Oh, I know,' Mrs Riddable had the air of explaining difficult truths to a young child. 'But the dean's own character would precipitate murder in the end. Trevor says.'

Theodora was beginning to dislike Canon Riddable on the strength of his family's quotations alone. 'What was wrong with his character?'

'He'd no parish experience and he was a terrible thruster.'

Theodora hardly liked to say that having parish experience was a positive disqualification for high office in the Anglican church and being a thruster was not uncommon and did not usually result in murder.

'Of course,' Mrs Riddable was scurrying on, 'Trevor will get his deanery in the end.'

So that was it. But surely Canon Riddable hadn't expected to be preferred to the deanery where he was a canon, that would be quite unusual.

'Bishops,' Mrs Riddable was following what was clearly a well-beaten track in her own mind, 'have such *tremendous* scope for doing good. Quite enviable really.'

Theodora forbore to say they also had considerable power, patronage and sheer privilege. The inability to distinguish between worldly power and spiritual power, Theodora had discovered, was as widespread among the clergy as the laity.

'I sometimes think Trevor feels time is rushing by. He'll be fifty next birthday. He's a Cancer and of course they are late developers.'

* * *

Sergeant Mules regarded the toes of the archdeacon protruding from beneath the red Jaguar.

'If you had a moment,' Mules murmured to the soles of the dirty trainers.

'Half a mo,' said Archdeacon Gold.

The car was raised dangerously on a couple of jacks, Mules noticed with disapproval. Presumably Parsonage Committees didn't run to providing pits in garages even for archdeacons. The Archdeaconry was out on the bypass. It had been built within the last ten years. The diocesan architects had used expensive materials to create an appearance of solidity. It was however only an appearance. The brass door fittings were hollow metal, the walls a mere brick facing on breeze blocks. It suited the archdeacon well. He liked it.

The archdeacon wiped his hands on a rag and stood leaning against the body of his car as though loath to be separated from it.

'I suppose it's about poor Vincent. I thought I'd said all I could about that one.'

Was it Mules' imagination or was the archdeacon hesitant? His normal manner, Mules guessed, was so jerky that it was difficult to tell if he was genuinely nervous.

'It's a matter of times initially,' Mules ventured.

'Well, as I've told you, I made my getaway

about ten to twelve. Brian Brace said how about a noggin, so I went to get the old girl,' he tapped the car, 'from the car park outside the magistrates' courts and followed old Brian down the road.'

'Arriving?'

'Say twelve ten.'

'Councillor Brace has a flat I believe.'

'He's got a pad at the end of Watergate for late-night sittings. That's in addition to his place out on Boundary Road. Enormous place,' the archdeacon added reverently.

'Then what?'

'Well we had one or two and I thought perhaps I'd better not risk the drive. Brian very decently offered me a billet.'

'So you stayed the night?'

'We turned in about oneish, I suppose. It's terribly well appointed, his little flat. It's got TV and a fridge in the spare bedroom.' The archdeacon's admiration knew no bounds.

'That must be very convenient,' said Mules heavily. 'Now, did you notice anything out of the ordinary happening during that evening or when you were leaving the Deanery? You didn't see anyone who shouldn't have been there? Any stranger?'

'To be quite honest,' the archdeacon gave the semblance of thinking, 'I can't remember too much. I think everything was shipshape.'

'Were you the last to leave the Deanery?'

'Yes. No. Er, well I think Trevor was

actually behind us. Yes,' strength of mind grew on him. 'Yes, come to think of it I'm pretty sure Canon Riddable was hanging back and having a word with Vincent as we left.'

'You didn't by any chance hear what he was saying?'

The archdeacon shook his head. 'Something about expert advice.'

'Expert advice on what? Who was giving advice on whom and about what?' Mules phrased his question precisely.

'Oh, I think Trevor was asking the dean for it. It'd have to be that way round, Sergeant.' The archdeacon grinned. 'But on what I haven't a clue.'

Mules shifted his ground. 'Do you happen to know if the dean had any financial worries, sir?'

'Vincent?' the archdeacon seemed genuinely surprised. 'Well, I suppose we're all a bit strapped for cash in the church. We don't do it for the pay, after all. Of course the big difficulties come in the upkeep of the cathedral. The fabric's crumbling and eating money in the process. We've simply got to get some cash from somewhere.'

'Was the dean very concerned about that?'

'No more than the rest of us. It's collective responsibility after all. Anyway with any luck the Hollow sale should fix it. Provided it comes off.'

'Is there any doubt of that, sir?'

‘Many a slip, Sergeant. And I can’t pretend it’s a popular move in certain quarters.’

‘Would that unpopularity provide a motive for murder, would you say?’

‘I can’t say what it would do in the mind of a madman, Sergeant.’

There seemed to be no more Mules could extract. He moved to take his leave. At the last his sense of responsibility overcame him. ‘You ought to get a pit dug, sir. It’s dangerous like that,’ he indicated the jacks at either end of the car chassis. ‘Could come crashing down on you any time.’

‘Can’t afford it, Sergeant. Got to live dangerously haven’t we?’

* * *

Stella read the article again, smoothing out the page of the *Bow Examiner* on the table in the Nissen hut in the Hollow. ‘New Age, New Religion’ ran the headline. Below that was a picture of the black lurcher standing and looking slightly embarrassed beside two white goats with the railway line in the background.

The article had been influenced by colour supplement journalism. ‘Number Two in our Series of Lifestyles’, its subheading announced, by ‘A. Pathfinder’.

‘*Oliver*

‘The community at the Hollow (literally on the

wrong side of the railway tracks) has hit the headlines because of the activities of its dynamic leader, Oliver Fresh. Oliver came to Bow in 1982. His own personal odyssey has given him wide experience of a variety of life styles both in the UK and abroad. Originally a village lad from Quecourt, he left school early and travelled the world. He's worked in Africa and on oil rigs. He was an apprentice saddler and knows about welding. Latterly he's turned his attention to archaeology. So it was the dream of a lifetime when he discovered the Bow St Aelfric Janus in the cathedral close. He is over the moon about it. "It confirms all I've striven for," he said when I interviewed him at his community centre in the Hollow.

'*Gods*

'"The Janus and the Hollow are the two things in the world I most care about," he said. And when I asked him, "Yes," he said, "I'm a deeply religious man. I think I'd call myself that. If you mean do I believe in God in the traditional sense of a big man up in the sky, then I'd have to say no. But I certainly do believe in gods, little sacred godlets who have a particular patch, like postmen. They're very powerful these little local gods. We neglect them at our peril. I think too we need to recognise there's a god inside us all. That's why I started the Hollow. When I came here, there was one Nissen hut and a lot of out-of-place water. Now look at it." He gestured to the neat allotments of onions, carrots and potatoes, flourishing between drainage ditches. The living quarters for the goats and hens. The LNER railway carriage and the two caravans.

'*Who and How*?

'Who comes here and how do they live? "Well, it's for anyone in need really. When I was in Africa I stayed with some Franciscan friars. It struck me they lived a completely harmonious life. They showed me what life should be like. They were so poor even I felt rich in comparison. At least I owned the clothes I stood up in. They lived from day to day and they fed and cared for and loved anyone who sought them out. I'd like to think we do something like that here. We don't refuse to house anyone, you know. They may not choose to stay with us because the price of a bed is work and not everyone wants to do that. But we never turn anyone away until they've refused."

'*Money*

'So how are they funded? Oliver himself works as a carpenter part time. "There's always plenty of work for a competent carpenter," he says. The other long stayers, Cathy and Reg Bean, also have regular work. She does part time with the special needs kids at the local primary school, he's a plumber with a firm of local builders. Then there are Kevin and Sean on community service. Kev knows about car maintenance, Sean's learning how to fence and paint and garden.

'They all keep their worldly needs to a minimum and work out the bills weekly. They take no state money but don't refuse contributions for the care of the animals if offered. The local schools pay small fees to bring their kids to help for a day and learn that milk doesn't come from bottles or honey out of jars. Many people, young and old, have found some sort of meaning in their lives by their contact with the Hollow men. "I hate to hear people say they're out of work and so they're useless. It's a real indictment of our society," Oliver says. "There's always work to do, skills to be learned and offered back. It may not be paid or recompensed. It may not make you successful or powerful, but there's always, as long as we draw breath, something we can all of us do."

'That's the sort of man Oliver Fresh is. And that's his lifestyle.'

And it was true, thought Stella. He did think that and he lived it day by day, with integrity and a sort of determined optimism. He knew the world was a terrible place; he knew he'd not win but he reckoned it was better to do the right thing and lose than to hedge your bets and be only half alive. She was grateful to him.

Thanks to him, she had regained her confidence. She had come to the Hollow paralysed by her guilt. Her emotions, indeed her very senses had been frozen. She remembered not being able to smell or taste anything. At her worst moments she had the impression she could not see people clearly. Bit by bit the work had restored her. She had literally come to her senses. Her first salvation had been food. The rituals of preparing and serving it had occupied her at the beginning. Later she had turned to planting and harvesting. She knew a great deal, she realised, about potatoes. From food she had progressed to weather. She began to be able to notice the basic stuff of the world. Earth, sand, mud, gravel, compost and water reawakened each of her senses. Their textures, their colours and smells literally grounded and confirmed her. Gradually pattern and harmony returned to her life and with it the ability first to notice and then to relate to people.

She looked round the room. The kitchen flowed into the living area which in its turn became a bedroom. At the far end a door led to Oliver's own room, part workshop, part bedroom. There was nothing rickety in the hut. Two rather elegant chairs of extreme solidity which Oliver had made stood on either side of the table. The bare boards of the floor were scoured to white cleanness. It had a look of a colonial homestead or perhaps the Amish dwellings she'd seen in America.

The sound of the car startled Stella from her self-appraisal. The lurcher bitch's hackle rose in an alarming brush on her shoulders and spine. Reluctantly, for she was a coward, she rose to a sitting position then, still baffled with sleep, flung back her head to give a deep contralto bark. Stella looked out of the window and a moment later the door was flung open.

'Stella, my dear.' The Reverend Canon Millhaven embraced her. 'Is all well with you? May I introduce a colleague of mine, Theodora Braithwaite. She's doing a placement with us on laity training. I felt she'd learn more from you and the Hollow than ever she will dashing round our cheery little meetings of retired bank managers.'

Stella saw a very tall woman of about ten years her junior, thirty or so, dark-haired, dark eyes set wide apart and strong features which you could not call pretty but might want to call handsome. Theodora saw the woman she had glimpsed from the railway carriage on her journey to Bow two days ago.

'How do you do?' they murmured in unison and realised that they were probably going to discover they were from the same stable.

'I'm going to leave Theodora with you. I've got to dash over to Quecourt to tidy one or two loose ends. Stella, show her what real religion is.'

Canon Millhaven swept her cloak around her and was gone. Theodora and Stella were left to make their own running.

'Are you fond of animals?' Stella was tentative.

'Very,' Theodora could reply with truthfulness.

'We've got a school party coming at two-thirty.'

'I'm less keen on children,' Theodora admitted.

'We should get round before they descend in full force.'

Stella led the way from the Nissen hut, the lurcher weaving through their legs to get out first.

'I read the article on you in the *Bow Examiner*,' Theodora began her exploration. 'I wondered who wrote it?'

'I think Oliver fed the information to someone at the *Examiner* office. I don't know who. I met the photographer though. He was very patient with the goats.'

'They seem to admire what you've achieved here.' Theodora said.

'It's more or less accurate. We don't aim quite as high as it suggests. I don't think any of us would claim to be offering a religion.'

'Canon Millhaven seems to think you are.'

'I suppose it depends a bit what you think religion is.'

What would you say?'

'For me it has to be any system of techniques which saves you, gets you through without murder or madness.'

Though this had the virtue of moral practicality, Theodora felt that it was a bit minimal.

'I think Erica's swayed by the shortcomings of her own institution,' Stella went on, 'so she overestimates the aims and perhaps the quality of what we can give here.'

'You mean she's exasperated by the Anglican Church.'

'Anything as elaborate and rich and many faceted and as political and powerful as that will have its problems,' Stella spoke with authority. 'It'll be trying to serve too many masters, for a start. Simplicity is all.'

'You sound as though you have experience of it?' Theodora's tone was so gentle in inquiry of this kind that there was no question of its seeming impertinent.

'I've known bits of it.' Stella was lulled by Theodora's whole presence. She'd forgotten what it might be like to talk to people, as she put it, of her own kind: the need not to explain, the certainty of being understood, the nuance which need not be elaborated. 'In fact I knew the dean, the late dean, slightly.'

They approached the far end of the Hollow where there was a paddock enclosing four fierce-looking Soay sheep, their dark woollen coats knotted and entwined with wisps of hay from the manger.

'They're a good breed to have with children in an urban area,' Stella said in her tour guide's voice. 'They're not afraid of children and they chase dogs. Mrs Bean's teaching one or two of the special needs children to card and spin the wool.'

'He seems to have been not much liked,' Theodora returned to the subject which had left neither of their minds.

'Vincent Stream lacked moral courage,' said Stella incisively, 'He wanted to satisfy convention rather than virtue.'

Theodora was about to pursue the topic. She wanted to hear more. She felt Stella's reservations might contain information which could help towards solving his murder. From the far end of the Hollow could be heard the shrill voices of a multitude of children.

'Would a lack of moral courage lead to his being murdered,' she inquired.

Stella looked towards the sheep. 'It might,' she said. 'It just might.' The noise of the school party swelled in the background.

Stella turned to her, as though she had reached some decision. 'Come back and see me when these have gone. Come tomorrow. Come early and stay to supper with the rest of us.'

Theodora could hope for no more. She unwound her legs from the lurcher's who had taken a fancy to her and strode back to the main entrance to the Hollow, swimming against a tide of excited children and harassed teachers.

* * *

'Your very good health, Miss Braithwaite,' said the young man formally, holding Theodora's sherry appreciatively between his fingers. Theodora watched him lean back in her armchair in the flat and saw how he liked being taken for himself and not as a role; what would it be, pupil, verger?

'May I congratulate you on a really excellent article in this quarter's *Church History Review*?' Nick began with pleasant courtesy. 'It really was a model of what such things ought to be.'

Theodora warmed to the youth. 'I gather that's going to be your line of country.'

Nick looked both modest and smug at the same time. 'Well, the nineteenth century isn't my period of course. I rather thought I might specialise in European mediaeval. They made such beautiful things and it would fit into the milieu of Oxford, wouldn't you say?' He smiled his charming smile.

Theodora agreed that it would. 'I've spent part of the day with Canon Millhaven,' she said by way of temptation.

'She's dire, isn't she?' Nick asked with enjoyment. 'When I was in choir school she used to come in once a week and teach us scripture. She was always on about blood as the foundation of religion. We did the goriest bits of the OT with her. Then she switched to pagan religion, with which she was clearly entirely at home. I forget whether she actually claimed it or whether we made it up about her, that Eric the Red was her ancestor. She's got a good deal dottier of late, wouldn't you say?'

'Well, I've nothing really to measure her against. This is my first meeting with her. What does she do?'

'She's been around a long time She goes back to before the time when she-deacons were fashionable. Way back when she did all the things the church ought to do. Cared for the sick and sorry, taught the children and visited the hospitals. It may have been a bit like being visited by a vampire. Then, when she-deacons became the flavour of the month, she was well placed to train them. So she did. Bishop Ronald liked the idea of a corps of Valkyries marching up and down the diocese, so he rather let her have her head. In the end, when they passed the Measure in '92, he gave her a residentiary canonry, partly to annoy chauvinists like Trevor Riddable.'

'I've met Mrs Riddable,' Theodora said. For a moment she thought Nick was going to say she too was dire. But he resisted the temptation so she pressed on. 'What's Canon Riddable like? I haven't met him yet.'

Nick looked down his elegant nose.

'Violent,' he said finally.

'What?' said Theodora, genuinely surprised by the young man's tone which was without banter.

'Well, all suppressed, mostly. But he's an absolute thug. He too taught at the King's School for a time. History, of a sort. In those days, before the '88 Act,' Nick was all modern historian, 'you could beat boys and he did. A parent complained and there was the threat of a court case. The bishop leaned a bit and the charge was dropped. But he has a temper and doesn't see why, as a residentiary canon, he should be expected to restrain it. Don't ever take his parking space. He parks behind you so you can't get out and goes in for verbal abuse when you return.'

Theodora sighed.

'It's a weedy garden, Miss Braithwaite. Nobody loves anybody else round here.'

'But the suffragan's all right, isn't he?' Theodora was forced to suggest. His kindness to her at the dean's party was fresh in her mind.

'Oh, yes. He's a gent. But it's not enough. Not by a long chalk.' Nick brooded for a moment on the inadequacy of gentility in the modern world.

'Archdeacon Gold?' Theodora insinuated gently.

'Good with engines. Hopeless with anything else. In fact he's seriously stupid.' Nick, enthroned in his Magdalen history scholarship, went on. 'Two abstract nouns in a sentence plus a double negative flummoxes him. Joined up writing never mind joined up thinking is quite beyond him. He picks up phrases from other people and strings them together and hopes they mean something. His political cronies from the Council run rings round him. He's desperate to plug the fabric fund's debt by selling off the Hollow land. Only to do that profitably he's got to have planning permission from the council. So he spends a lot of time toadying to oafs like Brian Brace. Not an edifying spectacle.' Nick managed to convey fastidious moral distaste.

'I gather the *Examiner*'s not in favour of that deal.'

'I think the *Examiner*'s quarrel with the cathedral clergy is actually rather more far-ranging.' Nick was judicious. 'The *Examiner* feels itself to be a champion of democracy and open government. The chapter isn't a type of rational, democratic system. It's simply a bastion of privilege. They're appointed on hearsay and supported unconditionally. They have a sinecure for life to live like nineteenth-century gentlemen. They're not scholars, their administration is done for them by laymen. They're too grand to do anything round the parishes. So they fill their diaries with smart ephemera and call themselves overworked. No wonder they get fractious and wander off down evil paths. They really ought to abolish the canons' freehold and make them all apply for their posts on five-year contracts. Then you might get some competence.'

Theodora rather liked the vigour of this. She thought it boded well for Nick's future career as an historian. However, since she had been familiar with cathedrals from her infancy it didn't add to her knowledge and so she brought him back to the matter in hand.

'They all seem a bit thrown by the Janus,' Theodora offered.

Nick returned to the fray with enjoyment. 'Don't they just? Isn't he splendid. He is so handsome, don't you think? You'd think they'd want to embrace him. Nothing like him's been found anywhere else in England. I had a very interesting conversation with Dunch. He wants the chapter to give him to his father's collection.'

'Which is where?'

'Part, I suspect the best part, he keeps at his house, Quecourt Manor. It's about ten miles out. Very splendid eighteenth century. Small with a joky front put on by Wyatt. I got in once with the Bow Antiquarian Soc. I was a bit too young to appreciate the finer points but I could see the quality. The rest of the collection's in the city museum in Watergate.'

'What will chapter do with it?'

'God knows. It's becoming a sort of touchstone of attitudes, have you noticed? The city people *like* him. But the chapter really can't cope. I suppose all those bones remind them of mortality about which they do not care to think. Gold wants him sold to pay off the cathedral's debts or else to make him into a rare show for the same purpose. Riddable wants him consigned to hell, which he probably thinks of as a geographical area roughly thirty foot below ground. I expect the suffragan thinks he should grace a gentleman's collection.'

'And the dean? What would he have wanted to do with him?'

'Well, who knows now?' Nick was suddenly sobered.

'What about the vergers?' Theodora inquired. 'Tristram Knight, for example.'

Nick cheered up, didn't say no to an offer of more sherry and shot his cuffs up his long wrists. 'Tris is all for him, of course. Tris is the best thing that's happened round here for ages.'

'Do I take it he got you your present post?' Theodora hazarded.

'Yes. Well. Yes. As a matter of fact he did. I mean I have this year before I go up. I do need cash quite badly. I very much want to go to the Midi for the Romanesque and I'm not the building site brickie type.'

Theodora looked at Nick's long fine boned hands and pale thin face and agreed.

'So eight months as a sub sub sub verger seemed ideal. He's been very kind to me.' There was emotion in his tone. 'Of course I more or less know the form from my choirboy years. But he showed me the ropes, kept me from the grosser errors. He's frightfully good fun too, I mean genuinely witty.'

Theodora noticed that Nick's sophistication seemed to have deserted him. He was, she surmised, in love.

'What's his background? He seems a cut above verger.'

'Oh we take all sorts.' Nick was laughing. 'I honestly don't know where he comes from or about his private life either. He's very close. He ...' Nick stopped suddenly.

Theodora raised an eyebrow.

'I mean he doesn't talk about his family or anything but he did once ... Well we used to play Rugby at Rugby and one morning I called for him at his lodgings and wound round a parcel of laundry was an old Rugbeian tie. Of course it might not have been his.'

'You didn't ask?'

'Good heavens no.'

Theodora warmed to the lad.

'What about the dean's murder?' Theodora again sought the direct approach. Since Nick seemed to be willing to be indiscreet on everything else, he might be prepared to say a word here too. But he was suddenly wary.

'How do you mean?'

'Have you theories about who might want to kill him?'

Nick adjusted his long legs from stretched to bent, lowered the rest of the sherry down himself and stood up.

'I'm terribly sorry,' he said suddenly much younger than his previous conversation might suggest. 'I said I'd stand in for Dennis at the Rotary Eucharist this evening. I must fly, if you'll forgive me.'

Theodora ran the glasses under the tap. Had the list of suspects lengthened? Nick had been quite good value on gossip but how far was he accurate? He clearly had strong likes and dislikes. He disliked Riddable, but then he'd only known him as a schoolboy and probably one who might have been rather difficult to contain. And what about Erica Millhaven? Was she really as dotty as Nick implied? She hesitated a moment on her return to the sitting room. It was a quarter past seven. Spruce would be here to compare notes at eight. She needed to get her thoughts in order and perhaps down on paper before they met. However there was one last job before the end of the day. She dialled the familiar London number.

'Geoffrey? Hello. Yes, I'm quite all right. You? Yes. Yes I know the nationals are running dead dean features all over the place. Yes, well only to be expected really. Look, could you do me a favour? A man called Tristram Knight. He was at your old school. About your age. Perhaps a bit younger. It might help to know the odd detail about his career.'

CHAPTER SEVEN

STRANGE GODS

'A chapter,' said Theodora glancing at Inspector Spruce across the polished mahogany surface of the sitting-room table, 'is the three or four clergy, called residentiary canons, plus a dean, who are responsible for running a cathedral.'

Spruce looked attentive. 'Who are they answerable to?'

'No one. And they're not trained and once in office they're practically irremovable and it's not always too obvious how they got their posts. It works through the patronage system.'

'So how do they spend their time?'

'In recent years,' Theodora was launched on a familiar path, 'their role has become unclear. Many cathedrals were originally monastic foundations. Monks were responsible for continuous worship in the cathedral, for scholarly activity, for looking after pilgrims and offering the church's hospitality to the needy. After the reformation, secular institutions took over many of their tasks. In the modern world cathedrals are faced with having to maintain very expensive buildings in a society where formal religious observance is no longer the norm. Chapters nowadays have to discover or invent what cathedrals are for. Some, like Salisbury, have gone for tourism, others have become museums, concert halls or conference and exhibition centres. Others again hold endless special services for different interest groups on the understanding that that links them with modern life. They've lost confidence in their ability to fulfil their original function.'

'Which is?'

'Bringing people into God's presence by the regular, prayerful celebration of a glorious liturgy, praying in public.'

'Why?' Spruce asked.

'Why what?'

'Why have they lost confidence in worship?'

Theodora sighed. 'Many reasons. It's partly to do with how we see causality in a scientifically orientated world. In such a world, prayer, which doesn't conform to scientific rules, looks odd. And to pray in public convincingly, you have to work at private prayer and that is the most enormous effort. It requires great self-discipline and it's utterly without worldly reward. No wonder the clergy prefer going in for politics or commerce.'

'Which way has Bow St Aelfric chapter chosen to go to justify its existence?'

'I rather think they are, as is often the case,

divided. The new dean quite properly in my view had in mind to go for liturgy with some trimmings. The canons, Riddable and Archdeacon Gold may not have agreed with him. The bishop suffragan has up to now held the ring. It's called a difference in churchmanship. The dean, suffragan and perhaps Canon Millhaven are in the Catholic tradition, the other two from the evangelical wing.'

Spruce clearly didn't want to go into this one. 'Are there any motives for murder in a set-up like that?'

'What are the motives for murder?'

'Fear, anger, greed, hatred.'

'An Old Testament list.'

'Contemporary vices.'

'So the inquiry has to be via motive?'

'In the end, of course. But initially it's opportunity we have to look at.' Spruce was incisive. He shook out the computer list on to the table. 'We checked the arrival time home of everyone who attended the dean's party.'

'But it need not have been anyone who attended the party,' Theodora objected.

'True. But if it was an outsider, there's the difficulty about gates. The Archgate, which is after all the only way into the close, is closed at this time of year after Evensong, about six-thirty. On Shrove Tuesday it was left open until all the dean's guests had come, then the second verger, what's he called?'

'Dennis, Dennis Noble, ' Theodora supplied.

'Right. Dennis locked it as he left at eight-thirty. It was unlocked again when the dean's guests began to leave round about a quarter to midnight. By the way,' Spruce broke off, 'why all this heavy, gaoling stuff?'

'The Ecclesiastical Insurance Office has started putting up the premiums of cathedrals which don't take their security seriously. We have to guard our worldly treasures.'

'So anyone who wanted to get into the close that evening by the Archgate would have to have either come in before eight-thirty or after about eleven-forty-five as the dean's guests were leaving. If they came in about eight and they weren't attending the party they would have to conceal themselves for four hours and then find a way out again after the murder.'

'When was the gate locked again after the guests had left?'

'The sub verger, Nick Squires, locked it when the last guest had gone, he says about five past midnight.'

'How about entry through one of the close houses which has a front door on to the street?'

'Actually they regard their front door as the one giving on to the close and speak of their back doors as the street doors.' Spruce was pleased with this piece of intelligence which he'd gleaned in the course of his inquiries amongst the clergy. 'An interesting clue perhaps to clergy attitudes?' He cocked an inquiring eye at Theodora.

She refused to rise. 'Well, how many do have *back* street doors?' Theodora asked.

'Only the Precentory and Canon Millhaven's Archgate rooms. The cathedral office doesn't nor do these buildings, that is, your flat nor the Deanery itself and nor does the choir school. We've checked both the buildings which do have street doors, and there's no sign of forced entry.'

'How about key holders?'

'Suprisingly few. Every house has a single key to the main, the Archgate. Keys to the doors on to the street are, naturally, in the keeping of those who live in those houses with street doors. That means that the Precentory and Canon Millhaven both have a key each for the Archgate and keys to their street doors. In addition the archdeacon has an Archgate key and there's one kept by the vergers in their office. You, and now I, have a key to this building which has, however, no street door. The choir school head keeps his Archgate key on his person and there are no others. The cathedral office is locked at five-thirty and the cleaners come in in the morning at seven when the vergers have opened the Archgate.'

'So,' said Theodora, 'if someone planned ahead to kill the dean, it would have been easier to come in early through the Archgate than to come in through the street doors of the

Precentory or Canon Millhaven's Archgate flat.'

'That would be my feeling.'

'There'd have to be two lots of concealing, one before the party and one after the murder until the gates were open at seven. Could that be done?'

'It'd be a long cold wait from one o'clock to eight and there are no signs of that having happened. I mean we didn't find a sleeping bag and a cache of sandwiches.' Spruce was ironic.

'I see you're set on it being someone at the party or anyway someone known to the dean,'

'It's the ritual aspect.' Spruce was intent and concentrated. 'The various signs round the body suggest he was killed near the cathedral and then dragged across the wet grass and placed,' he repeated with emphasis, 'placed, not just let go, but laid out with care, in front of the Janus.'

Theodora nodded in comprehension. She too had to acknowledge that, sickening though she felt it to be, it looked as though the murderer had to be someone who knew the dean, who was in fact within the church in the diocese of Bow St Aelfric.

There was a pause. She glanced across at Spruce's face. Its planes of bone were illuminated by the subdued lighting from the single lamp. His dark eyes and brows contrasted with the premature whiteness of his hair. He looked alert, sympathetic and intelligent. The fire roared in the grate, the heavy velvet curtains were drawn across the single window. A glass of sherry stood at their elbows. Theodora shuffled her notes on the mahogany surface. Spruce looked up. 'To me,' he said. 'it's an intellectual puzzle. To you it's the church in danger. I'm sorry. I do recognise that.'

'We must get it cleared up. No point in concealment or evasion. The church does too much of it.'

They smiled. Respect was mutual. Spruce looked at his watch. 'I've asked Sergeant Mules to look in in about half an hour with an Indian take-away. I hope that's OK? I did a couple of years in Hong Kong and I find English versions of Chinese not so much subtle as insipid.'

'Let's push on to the times,' Theodora suggested.

'The dean's watch had its face smashed as he fell and the hands stopped at ten past one. So that fixes the time of death. Of the clergy at the party, the suffragan and his wife got back to Quecourt at twelve-thirty according to his housekeeper. Archdeacon Gold went on for a final drink with a couple of his local politician cronies, Messrs Ferret and Brace, and spent the night at the flat of one of them. Canon Riddable ...'

Theodora leaned forward. 'Canon Riddable,' she prompted.

'According to Mrs Riddable they both returned together at about twelve-thirty. Of course they walked home across the close.'

'His children,' Theodora said flatly, 'or at least one of them thinks he returned much later than that.' She told him what Ben had said that morning on the stairs. 'And,' she went on, 'the eldest girl says she saw the dean near the Janus heading towards the cathedral at a quarter to one.'

'So,' said Spruce, 'if Ben is right, Canon Riddable was returning at half past one. Of course the child could be wrong or Riddable could be returning after some perfectly innocent activity.' Spruce raised his head and looked at Theodora's doubtful face. 'Hang on a minute. How does the clock strike?'

Theodora nodded. 'There are three ones,' she said. 'The cathedral clock strikes one stroke for twelve-thirty, one and one-thirty.'

'Oh God,' Spruce groaned. 'Which did little Riddable think he was hearing when he says his dad returned later than twelve-thirty?'

'One o'clock, I think,' Theodora responded. 'But equally he could have meant one-thirty.'

'I'll have to get a WPC and one of the parents to question young Riddable obviously. But let's see if we can get at it any other way first. Motive?' he said as though passing her a dish.

Theodora told him what Nick had said about Riddable. 'Though, of course,' she concluded, 'it doesn't provide motive, only possible temperament.'

'What else do you know of Riddable?'

'He started off as a church historian.'

'Not a crowded market,' Spruce hazarded.

'More popular than it once was. In fact I'd say the standard is rather higher there than in theology proper. However,' Theodora caught the look in Spruce's eye and swung back to the matter in hand, 'he published a couple of things in *Church History Review*. As it happens I have read him both times. The first was rather poor, on the economic basis of the sects in Cromwell's army. Lots of sweeping generalisation without much evidence. The second one was markedly better, on nonconformity in the nineteenth century. It looked like the sketch for a longer work but it had a lot of good detailed stuff in it.'

Spruce's eyes were glazing. 'Murder,' he said.

'Yes, yes.' Theodora felt he should trust her. 'I'm coming to that. After the last article, must be six years ago now, he's published nothing. And his wife said'—Theodora remembered Mrs Riddable's words—'he's given up historical scholarship.'

'Well?'

Theodora was hesitant. 'I did hear a bit of gossip. You know how the clergy are and of course scholars do tend . . .'

'The point being,' Spruce was almost tart.

'You see,' Theodora ventured, 'it was noticed by several people at the time. The difference in calibre between the two articles was so marked.'

'I don't see what you're driving at,' Spruce said with exasperation.

'The point is that Riddable's father was a church historian, rather a respectable one, specialising in the nineteenth century.'

'Do you mean he'd used Papa's stuff and didn't bother to mention it to the editor?' Spruce took her point instantly. He was back on home ground now. Theft he knew about. 'Could the dean have known?'

'I think I could probably find out,' Theodora volunteered. She thought of Ivan Markewicz who edited the *Review*. She thought too of her great uncle, Canon Hugh who had known the original gossip. 'Leave it with me.'

'Right. I'll have another go at Riddable about times. He's clearly got some accounting to do. My only reservation is, if I do question the lad, is he going to stick to his tale if his pa or ma's there?'

Theodora thought of the tough little crew of Riddable children. Were they, she wondered, exhibiting symptoms of victim behaviour, or had they got their parents worked out and the strategies in place for dealing with them and surviving. Those children, though different, were very close to each other, Theodora felt. 'I'll have a go there too, if the opportunity arises. I rather took to the middle boy, the one who found the Janus.'

'From the clergy list that leaves the diocesan bishop. I faxed Nebraska. He's staying at the university there with his son. He states he and Mrs Holdall motored straight home to Little Manor at Fenny Drain because they had to catch a flight at six the following morning. As it happens, a panda car saw him arrive about one o'clock.'

'Why did it take him so long to get home? Little Manor's just outside the town.'

'He dropped Sir Lionel Dunch off at Quecourt first.'

'Pity. I rather hoped Dunch . . .' Theodora caught herself up. That was aterrible thing to say. 'So Dunch is out of the list too.'

'The last of the clerical list is Canon Millhaven. I gather she was asked to the party but it was a late invitation.'

Like Carrabosse, Theodora thought. 'I didn't see her there.'

'She told me that she felt too tired and in the end decided not to go. She affirms,' Spruce turned up the computer swathe again, 'that she did not see any reason to inform the dean she was not coming since he had already cancelled an engagement with her earlier in the week.'

Yes, thought Theodora. Tit for tat. 'Anyone to corroborate that?'

'No. But if she had been about, wouldn't she have been seen? She's rather a noticeable figure.'

'Well, someone was about in the close and wasn't seen. Apart from the God.' Theodora realised she was becoming light-headed. 'Which god was about in the quad?' she murmured.

'Would she have a motive?' Spruce inquired.

'There was no love lost clearly. But I don't know of anything very specific.'

'What is she exactly? I mean apart from being a female residentiary canon?' Spruce's tone was ironic.

'She's immensely senior,' Theodora replied, 'in both clergy terms, which means having been in orders a long time, and also in terms of the work she's actually accomplished. She's served long and hard.' Theodora was positive. 'She cares about the laity and single-handed, with no help at all from the hierarchy except in the last couple of years, she put in place a lay education programme well before that sort of thing was fashionable. But, of course she is still in deacon's orders.'

'Which means?' Spruce inquired.

'She can't celebrate at the Eucharist or bless or absolve in the course of the liturgy.'

'Wouldn't that be difficult for a residentiary canon?'

'Yes,' Theodora admitted. 'It would. It is. Canons usually take a month at a time when they're "in residence," that is, when they're responsible for the whole of the cathedral's worship including celebrations of the Eucharist. You can get round it by using bread and wine which has previously been consecrated by someone in priest's orders and reserved. And that, I gather, is what Canon Millhaven did. But it wouldn't be popular as a solution.'

'Who would object?' Spruce was curious.

'The dean certainly, I'd have thought, wouldn't care for a woman celebrating with reserved sacrament.'

'But it wouldn't be a motive for murder would it?'

Theodora thought of the blood spilt down the ages on theological points a good deal less central than this one. 'I suppose not. At least amongst the sane.'

'So deacons orders are second best?' Spruce said.

'Not to me,' Theodora said firmly.

'Will you ever be priested?' He turned the unfamiliar word over in his mouth. He liked other people's language.

Theodora turned her head towards the fire light. 'I don't honestly care too much,' she said. 'I'm perfectly content in deacon's orders. There's very little that I want to do and think needs doing which I can't do as a deacon. If we aren't offered the priesthood freely, generously by the whole church, then it would be vulgar to start shouting for it.' She wondered whether she trusted Spruce enough to tell him about

Millhaven's speaking to the cathedral dead.

'She talks to the dead,' she said after a pause.

Spruce took it in his stride. 'When and where?'

'I gather in the cathedral. I inferred, though she did not say so explicitly, at night.'

'Would the dean know?'

'I've no idea.'

'Would you say she was unbalanced?'

Theodora considered in her scrupulous way. 'Half of her is sane and eminently competent. She has sudden lapses, like the talking to the dead. Also she has bees in bonnets. For example she's keen on the Hollow community.'

There was a peal on the ancient door-bell far below. 'Supper', said Spruce hungrily.

Laying out their meal, Sergeant Mules showed himself thoroughly domesticated. Spruce, who had been at work since eight-thirty that morning unremittingly questioning, planning, checking, noting, calculating, gave no sign of tiredness. Mules, who had been working equally hard, was the same. He had something of the air of a machine, a small efficient tractor perhaps. Theodora reflected on the different attitudes to work of senior clergy compared with laity. Best not pursued she felt.

'The Hollowmen,' Spruce resumed a third of a way through a chicken tikka. He looked questioningly at Mules.

'Not liked locally. Do good work with

community service referrals from the courts. It's grown a lot over the last four years. Seems to fill a need.' Mules was laconic. It was his forte. Never waste a word. He crumpled his poppadom and stared into his Kingfisher.

'Fill us in,' Spruce invited.

'They've been there about seven years. Started with nothing. Creation out of nothing as it were. Good vegetables. Some of the best I've seen in onions and onions aren't that easy. Chickens are all right. Animals I don't know about.' Mules was thorough, Theodora thought. Would he go for buildings next or people?

'The buildings were a couple of Nissen huts and a caravan. They've put them in order beautifully. That chap Fresh is a good carpenter. I'll give him that. The difficulty as far as the locals are concerned is that they don't fit into any category. They aren't gypos. Fresh's woman is high class. The Beans aren't but they do a good job. They aren't exactly a religious community either, so they get called new agers or hippies. But they aren't. The quantity of washing proves that.' Mules was triumphant.

'I didn't realise the archaeologist Fresh was one of them.' Theodora was genuinely interested. 'Now the dean certainly didn't like him.' She filled them in on her overheard conversation between the dean and Fresh and mentioned what she had learned at the party and from Mrs Riddable about the chapter's attitude to the Janus

'Is the Janus connected to the murder?' Mules was clearly fulfilling his role of asking the blunt question.

'If Fresh is a suspect there might be a motive there. If Millhaven is unbalanced there might be a motive there too. I really can't see any space for Mrs Riddable's notion that the powers of the Janus are in themselves without human agency responsible for murder.' Spruce changed his tikka for a grilled bone.

'Was Fresh at the party?' Theodora inquired.

'Not officially,' Spruce answered. 'But . . .' He turned to Mules who in his turn took out a swathe of computer continuous.

'One of the vergers, Noble, says he thought he saw him before he went home at eight-thirty as he was locking the gates.'

'How sure was he?'

'Not very. He saw someone near the Janus and I suppose having seen Fresh there all day he may have made the inference that that was who it was.'

'Why didn't he turn him out of the close?' Theodora asked.

'He walked across towards the statue but when he got there he'd gone. So he assumed that he'd been asked to the dean's party.'

'The vergers. How far have we got in questioning the vergers?' Spruce turned to

Mules.

'I've had a preliminary go with all three. The old man, Noble, as we know left at eight-thirty last night and returned at seven-thirty this morning to find the body. He lodges at the pub flat in the Aelfric Arms on the corner of Archgate and Watergate. He drank there till closing time. The boy, Nicholas Squires, helped at the dean's party and left with the head verger Tristram Knight. Knight as head verger had the verger's key to Archgate. Knight got back to his lodgings about one, he says. Squires lives with his dad off the bypass and he confirms he was home by one.'

Spruce looked across at Theodora. 'You were going to see Nick.'

Theodora nodded. 'He didn't say anything which would contradict that.' When she'd tried to question Nick about the dean's murder, he'd simply left. On the other hand she had learned at least something about the chapter and its relationships from him.

'How do we stand with Fresh?'

'Since he wasn't at the party I haven't got round to him yet,' Mules answered. 'I've got him on tomorrow's list.'

Spruce seemed to make a decision. 'Let's call it a day. For tomorrow on the front row of suspects we have Riddable, Millhaven, Fresh. I'll have a go at Riddable and Millhaven. You,' he looked questioningly at Theodora, 'I think you kindly said were going to try for the

Riddable children again. We'd better see Fresh. Mules, you have first go and I'll come in later. Finally, of course, we need to know much more about the dean's background. I've got the Met checking the London bit but I rather think he may not have a criminal record. So,' he looked again at Theodora, 'we shall be very glad indeed of anything which you could produce through your network.'

'I have the odd feeler out,' Theodora admitted. 'The other thing is, ought we to go through the dean's things?' She hated saying this but the ideas which were forming in her mind impelled her.

Spruce was quite sensitive enough to know what she felt. 'Yes, I've got the keys from the suffragan. Like you he wasn't keen. It's amazing what the clergy think they have the power to stop the police doing. I thought I'd have a go in the morning before I do Riddable and Fresh. I'd be awfully grateful if you felt able to give me a hand.'

Theodora nodded. He rose and Mules followed him. 'Let's see if the key they've given us to the Archgate works.'

Together they clumped down the carpetless stairs and came out into the moonlit close. The Janus seemed to have grown taller. It had been chocked up more securely on its scaffold of planks. The cloak or black polythene had been removed and the splendid head and torso rose up to dominate the space. By instinct they moved together across the turf towards it. The long black shadow stretched out across the ground to meet them. There was a glint of light on the grass in front of the face turned towards the city. Theodora bent down. On two bits of stone had been placed a shallow metal dish. Experimentally she ran her finger round the rim and put it to her lip. 'Milk and honey,' she said. 'Goat's milk, to be precise.'

CHAPTER EIGHT

CATHEDRAL CLOSE

The smell was of good quality incense mixed with bacon. Theodora knew and appreciated both. She tapped on the vestry door.

Tristram Knight was folding clerical vestments. Stoles in the colours of the Church's year, green, red, white, purple ran through his hands. Theodora noticed he had a needle and cotton in the lapel of his tweed jacket. The vestry was small and intimate, almost den-like. The door of one of the cupboards was partly open. In the bottom of it were what looked like sleeping bags. On the back of its door had been fixed a small mirror and a shelf of brushes, combs and razors. There was an open fire in a Victorian grate. Presses reached to the ceiling on two sides. On the table was an ancient

Remington typewriter the like of which Theodora had not seen since her vicarage childhood. Over the fire was a wooden crucifix. It felt like a wholly different and self-sufficient world from the cathedral proper above it. It crossed Theodora's mind to wonder whether it was supporting or subverting that edifice.

'I'm looking for Nick,' Theodora said.

'Fiddling with his favourite toy, the sound machine aloft, and then off until Evensong.' Tristram did not look at her.

'I looked in the cathedral but didn't see him.'

Tristram changed to folding cassock albs and stacking them neatly on the table. His movements were rapid, expert, charged with energy. His oddly set head made it easy for him to look over other people's. He often seemed, Theodora realised, to be addressing an audience unseen by his interlocutors. Since Tristram did not seem disposed to offer help, Theodora tried again.

'Has the dean's death made life difficult for you here?'

'It's increased the numbers attending services. As you doubtless saw, the eight o'clock Eucharist this morning reached double figures for the first time outside a major festival.'

Theodora, who had attended the early service, had no means of measuring the usual turnout. 'Ghoulishness or a genuine turning to God?'

'I would not presume to penetrate human hearts,' Tristram smiled at his unseen audience. 'You must have gathered that the dean will not be much missed in many quarters.'

'Why?' There was no point, Theodora felt, in beating about the bush with this subtle snake. If she was to get a feel for motives, never mind the opportunities, she would have to blunder about a bit and see what was thrown up.

Tristram suddenly expanded as though he felt the need to run off the lead for a bit. Had he bottled up emotions too long, Theodora wondered.

His high, clear voice sounded as though he were lecturing a group of students in elementary theology. 'It's a question of charity, isn't? Without which we are told we are nothing worth. Charity and sincerity. Let all your discourse be sincere, your converse as the noon day clear.'

'And the dean's wasn't?'

'You saw him at his party. He found it difficult to relate to his equals. He needed to feel he was in control and that everyone acknowledged it.'

'You sound as though you'd suffered from that.' As soon as she said it she realised she'd made a false move. Tristram spared her a single glance from his fishy eye.

'He thought of vergers in a Trollopian mode of resourceful NCOs who would wash his car and be glad to do a bit of buttling for a fiver on the side.'

'You didn't see your duties in those terms?'

'I have absolutely no objection to turning my hand to any task. Nothing demeans the pure spirit.' Tristram smiled again to the audience just above Theodora's head. 'I spent five years at a public school which still expected lower school boys to fag. No, what annoyed the dean was that I clearly didn't regard him as my superior, morally, intellectually or socially. He simply happened to have a different job from me. I wasn't deferential. He couldn't cope with me.'

'How did it show itself?'

'I doubt if I should have lasted much longer here if he'd lived.'

'Would you have minded?'

'It's convenient for me at the moment. I have my own reasons for wanting to retain my connexion with the Church.'

Theodora glanced at the Remington . . . 'It's good copy, isn't it?'

'If I ever wanted to write, I think I could hardly do better,' Tristram replied gravely. 'Few would believe the extremities of behaviour of its senior professional members.'

It was Theodora's turn to smile. 'I would . . . I was born into a clerical family. However, I'm wasting your time. I'd better see if I can find Nick.'

*   *   *

Henry Clement, the suffragan bishop, the most senior cleric in the diocese in the absence in America of the diocesan bishop, put the *Bow Examiner* down on his desk. In spite of the croscuses and snowdrops prettily showing beneath the wych elm in the centre of his view from the Quecourt library window, he felt as though a huge weight was pressing on his head and chest. All his life, from his earliest manhood, he had laboured without sparing himself to support and extend the Church's work as he had been brought up to understand it. He'd graduated from participating in to presiding over meetings without number, from PCCs and Deanery synods, church lads and industrial missions to general synod committees and cathedral chapters. His gentleness, his modest scholarship, his seamless courtesy and, he admitted it, his family connexions had made it almost inevitable that he should end a bishop. He had not had to strive or jockey. He wore his rank most becomingly. There was no trace of vanity or pomposity. He had no taste for administration but he had cultivated a life of prayer which irrigated his every choice and utterance. He knew himself respected, even loved. Intellectually he had never doubted the central truths of Christianity that salvation can come only through the imitation of Christ in innocent suffering.

He conceived the Church as the natural home of the good-willed and well-mannered. There was no problem which could not be solved by recourse to one or both of these. Of course he had noticed that times had changed. People were less mannerly than previously. This had not seemed to him to require an alteration in his own excellent conduct. It occurred to him sometimes that society wanted the Church to change but he could not think in what ways it could or ought to do so, without bringing the whole traditional edifice tumbling down. Did the Church's social and political structures reflect the religious teachings of its founder? Of late he had wondered. He looked again at the *Examiner's* offending article. What was it all for if the modern world treated the Church like this?

'Death of a Dean Ushers in New Age' ran the headline. It was not quite an obituary, though passing reference was made to the tragic and unsolved death of the dean. But, in the main, the article was an attack on the cathedral as a repository of Christian values. 'What do they do?', was the recurring theme of the writing, where the 'they' clearly referred to the chapter. 'Do they comfort the bereaved? Do they house the homeless? Do they teach the ignorant? Do they foster scholarship? Are they patrons of the arts?' The writer hammered on, placing his resounding 'no' in capital letters in answer to each question. 'Do they live the simple lives of the Franciscan, setting us an example of humility and poverty and inspiring the world by the quality of their own lives?' The writer didn't even bother to put a 'no' in answer to this one. 'Do they offer regular and uplifting worship to Almighty God?' his peroration thundered. 'Not recently, as those who attended the late dean's installation will remember. What they are quite good at is filling in their entries in *Who's Who* and paying their subscriptions to the Athenaeum. They have yet to learn that rushing from meeting to meeting is not the same as work. They fill their diaries but not their minds,' the author concluded with a Churchillian flourish. 'They fill their coffers by persecuting the innocent and powerless. Our readers will recall that the strip of land, on which the little group of do-gooders called the Hollowmen are encamped, is due to be sold over their heads by the owners. Those owners are the dean and chapter of Bow St Aelfric cathedral. They intend to put up some much unneeded office blocks. It all seems a long way from Jesus of Nazareth. Do we need new blood in the Church of England?' the writer ended by inquiring. 'Do we even need a new religion? Has the time of the Janus come?'

The bishop blanched. Then with unwonted decisiveness he picked up the telephone, managed after only two attempts to dial the right number and wondered if it would be at all possible for Miss Braithwaite to spare him a moment of her valuable time. Had she by any chance seen the article in the *Bow Examiner*?

Theodora, ensconced happily with a coffee cup beside a large wood fire in the clerical flat, a pile of Canon Millhaven's documents in front of her, pulled the paper across the table. Her eye skimmed the column. Good undergraduate stuff, she thought. She rather admired the rhetorical devices. Plenty of vigorous hatred there as well as one or two pertinent questions.

'I wondered whether you'd made any progress in the matter of discovering the authorship of these things?' For the bishop, the tone was almost sharp.

Theodora was glad she was on the phone and did not have to deal with the eye contact as well. 'I have a theory,' she answered cautiously.

'To what effect?'

'I think it may be a member of the cathedral staff.'

'By staff, I take it you do not mean clergy.'

'No,' said Theodora, 'I don't think it's one of the clergy.' She forbore to say that with the dean dead she hardly thought any of them could turn a sentence to match those of 'Pathfinder'.

'I see. That does indeed account for his knowledge, though it does not excuse his ingratitude.'

It occurred to Theodora to wonder for what the non-clergy staff were supposed to be grateful. Beautiful buildings perhaps but when you'd said that, you'd said it all.

'Look,' Theodora said, stung to honesty and plain speaking in the light of the bishop's skimpolery. 'First, I can't for certain prove what I suspect. It all depends on a typewriter face. Secondly, what do you want to do with him or her if you do know who they are? Thirdly, if, as I think likely, this may be a last blast, why not let well alone?' She did not add the fourth possibility, that he should actually address the criticism made in the articles and at the very least consider the point of view of the unbelieving world.

There was a silence while the bishop chewed this one over. Finally he said, 'You mean it might do the church more harm than good to uncover the writer?'

Theodora mentally congratulated him on his grasp. 'It's a possibility,' she admitted, 'would you not say?'

'But what if these attacks are connected with the dean's murder?'

Theodora could hear the reluctance in the bishop's tone. She commended his courage in facing the possibility. Say he was right, say someone, a madman, a neurotic, was writing these things, say the dean had discovered his or her identity and the person simply slit the dean's throat to avoid being unmasked.

Theodora caught herself up. The tone of the articles though passionate was rational, eminently sane. She had to admit it was no more than was being said by the enlightened in both parish and diocese ... She felt it safe therefore to say, 'It's simply, as I said, that I lack proof.'

'Did you say something about a typeface?' The bishop's tone was milder as though he'd ceased to blame her for the insolence of the writer.

'Yes.'

'I have a typed copy of the "View from a Pew" article,' said the bishop briskly. 'I picked it up from the new machine in the cathedral office on Monday.'

The devil you did, Theodora did not say. 'Might I have a look at it? I could call this afternoon if you were agreeable.'

'I am entirely at your disposal,' said the bishop whose diary, though not it was fair to say his mind, was empty.

* * *

Canon Riddable gazed at Inspector Spruce with disbelief. Why wasn't the man frightened of him? Riddable had always found that if he shouted loud enough and thumped the table hard enough, people (pupils, laymen, fellow clergy) had scuttled for cover. He had brought throwing tantrums up to an art form. It served him as a pattern for most human intercourse. Mrs Perfect could have told them. For some reason he couldn't at all fathom, on this occasion the technique hadn't worked. He had invoked his tutelary deities, the bishop, the chief constable, to no effect. The man just went on gazing at him, repeating the same horribly threatening question. Perhaps the fellow hadn't understood that he was a residentiary canon.

'You'll appreciate, Inspector,' his tone was almost forgiving, 'that I'm a member of chapter here. I'm a residentiary canon. I have,' he smiled deprecatingly, 'a certain amount of clout.'

Spruce nodded, his face expressionless. 'The time of your return from the dean's party ...' he began again.

Riddable interrupted him. 'I'm simply not prepared to allow this line of questioning to continue. I find it totally unacceptable.' Surely the fellow would get the point.

Spruce continued to gaze at him. 'We're investigating a man's murder, Canon. Your dean's murder to be precise. Times are very important. You'll appreciate that. Now, your time of return from ...' he began again.

Riddable leaned forward suddenly and banged the desk with the flat of his hand. 'I thought I had made myself clear. If you suppose this sort of behaviour will get you anywhere, you're living in cloud cuckoo land.'

He leaned back with finality, appearing to suppose the interview was now at an end.

Spruce thought how very pleasant it would be to take the oaf by the ears and shake his eyes out. He caught himself up. How contagious violence was. So often in his career he'd seen the beer glass shoved into the face, the boot swinging towards the head on the ground. All of a piece, bullying, only a matter of degree. It starts behind the bike sheds and ends apparently in canons' stall. He was disconcerted, though, to find it in the Church when it was his own profession which was so often accused of practising it. He gave no appearance of having noticed anything odd in Canon Riddable's behaviour. 'You say you returned to the Precentory with Mrs Riddable at twelve-ten.'

Riddable rose to his ungainly feet. He was breathing heavily as he swerved towards the door. In front of it stood Sergeant Mules, foursquare. For a moment it looked as though the canon might take a swing at him. Mules was hoping he might. Riddable said without turning round, 'Tell your man to get out of my way.'

Spruce allowed quite a long pause, judging that the adrenalin which the canon had summoned to work himself up to make a physical gesture would evaporate. Then he said very quietly, 'There's a police car outside, Sergeant. We'll be taking Canon Riddable to the station for questioning.'

Riddable hesitated. Spruce, who knew that if he let up the pressure for a moment, the canon would bounce back like Toad, said, 'I take it you have no objection to coming down to the station to help us with our inquiries?'

'Look,' said Riddable, his tone suggesting he was making allowances for a too importunate curate, 'I can give you ten minutes' maximum. I'm absolutely up to my eyes. The diary,' he gestured, 'is choc-a-bloc.' He shook his head as though burdened with a cabinet minister's commitments. He sat down again. Mules relaxed.

'Well now, Canon,' Spruce too had changed his tone. It suggested he was dealing with a backward child unable to make connexion at the abstract level but with whom he was prepared to be patient. How much of Riddable's temper was simulated, he wondered, and how much real, the inadequate reaction of an inadequate man. He felt sudden pity for him. How appalling to be Riddable. Had he killed the dean? He had the temper but not the guts. Certainly not the guts to drag the body from the Deanery door and lay it out in front of the Janus. However, in the light of what Theodora had said there might be a motive worth probing and he was not disposed to let Riddable off the hook again, given his nasty manners. He'd see how far he could push him about times, then he'd turn to the other matter.

Carefully Spruce took him through the times.

'You were seen returning to the Precentory later than the time of twelve-ten.'

'By whom?'

'I'm not at liberty to disclose that,' Spruce was parodying Riddable's diction. He rather enjoyed that. But in the end, even with the threat of being taken to the station hovering unspoken between the two of them, the most that Riddable would agree to was that he'd left Mrs Riddable at the Precentory and gone back to see the dean about a chapter matter.

'What time did you finish your interview with the dean?'

Riddable agreed to twelve-thirty.

'What did you go back to see the dean about at that time of night?'

'Chapter business.'

'What business?' Spruce pressed. For a moment it looked as though there was going to be a return to the I-am-not-prepared-to line. Then Riddable thought better of it. Riddable was beginning to mumble. His secretary could have told Spruce that when Riddable mumbled he'd given in.

'You'll appreciate, Inspector, that the dean was new in office, new to his post. I had to put him right on one or two points, senior clergy and all that.' Riddable's tone suggested that the conversation had moved on to a more socially intimate level.

'What about?' Spruce asked again. Riddable looked desperate. 'Service times,' he said at last. 'I had to set him right on the times of the services.'

Spruce looked incredulous. 'How?'

'He wanted to lengthen them,' said Riddable with distaste.

Spruce allowed himself a smile of disbelief. Then he pulled a file towards him and took out the note he'd received from Theodora just before he'd started the interview. If he couldn't quite clinch the affair with Riddable in the matter of times, perhaps he could do something in the line of motive. Theodora's note read, 'Ivan Markewicz, editor of *CHR*, says Dean Stream advised rejection of Riddable's article on grounds of poor quality. Ivan had communicated this to Riddable.' Spruce took his time to read the note through again. He was determined to control the tempo of the interview. He guessed Riddable felt most comfortable making his point, or hurling his abuse and then marching out before he had to listen to alternative views. He's been thoroughly spoilt, Spruce thought suddenly, reverting to the judgements of his childhood.

'Am I right in thinking, Canon, you had a common interest with the dean in church history?' Spruce's tone was smooth and inviting. Only the most obtuse would have supposed that he had changed the subject.

'Well, the dean was hardly a scholar, of course.' Riddable's tone was hearty and relieved. He clearly felt he'd made a safe landing.

'But you had resumed scholarly work yourself recently after something of a gap?'

'One never really gives up those sorts of interests, Inspector. I'm sure you find that yourself.'

Since Spruce had no scholarly activity which would have claimed the attention of Canon Riddable, he could only interpret this extraordinary remark as a wish to make amends, to include him in as one of the chaps.

'I understand you recently sent an article to the *Church History Review*.'

Riddable seemed to find nothing extraordinary in the Inspector knowing this. He probably assumed, Spruce thought, that the entire world was awaiting his next publication with bated breath.

'They invited me to put together a short paper for them and I felt it was the least I could do. They're always desperate for stuff, you know. Though of course they have very high standards.'

Make up your mind, Spruce thought. Either they take anything or they don't.

'Did you ever discuss your scholarly work, your articles, with the dean?' Spruce inquired.

'I doubt if Vincent would have been able to follow the drift. Some of the material's very technical.'

'So there was no question of the dean's having vetted the article for *CHR* or of your having discussed the work with him?'

Riddable laughed heartily. 'Absolutely not, Inspector.'

Spruce reckoned he'd got all he was likely to. 'You've been more helpful than you might think,' he said with a sudden unnerving wide smile to Riddable. Then to make his day he added, 'I'll be in touch with you again very soon.'

* * *

'I had to come down pretty heavily on that policeman.' Riddable told his wife at lunch. 'He needed a kick in the pants, which I was very happy to give him.' He chewed his fish finger thoughtfully. Then, feeling perhaps that Mrs Riddable had not seized his point, he added, 'I'll have to see his chief constable about him. I've known Ronnie for years, of course.'

He sometimes told Mrs Riddable facts of which she was already aware. It seemed to make them more factual if he told her them again.

'I shot him down in flames,' he went on complacently. 'As you know, I shoot from the hip.' His temper was restoring as he talked and chewed. 'I shot him down in flames and rode off into the sunset.' He concluded, now made over.

*   *   *

Stella stared into the candle flame and then let her eye travel beyond it. The Hollowmen and their guests were gathered for their evening. They were twelve in all. The members of the community had washed and changed, taken off their shoes and assembled in the kitchen Nissen hut, Stella's and Fresh's. They sat in a circle, some cross-legged, some on the slatted stools which Oliver had constructed. On a low round table in their midst a single tall candle burned.

Besides Oliver and herself there were Mr and Mrs Bean, Erica Millhaven and her tall guest Theodora Braithwaite, Sean and Kevin and their probation officer, a fair diminutive Scot called Gavin, Kevin's current girl, an Afro-Caribbean called Jewel, and Miriam and Matthew Rosen, accountants both and early supporters of the enterprises at the Hollow.

The daylight, after hanging around for a bit as though not quite knowing what to do with itself, had by seven o'clock in early March faded. Through the uncurtained window Stella could see the arc lamps of the railway and the encroaching building site. The evening was mild. The smell of damp earth came in through the open door and near at hand a blackbird experimented with his spring calls. Stella's fears, first about the guilt-ridden past, then about the future, food, (would it be all right, would there be enough?) came to her as they regularly did at this moment. But now after three years she was strong enough to catch them as they came and watch them as they dropped away into limbo. She brought her gaze back to the candle flame and let out her breath. In these small nightly pockets of calm and silence she knew she was safe: silence saved, weather saved, friends saved.

Erica Millhaven stared into the flame. Through it she saw Oliver and Stella sitting side by side on the other side of the bare room, their heads close together and silhouetted like a double cameo. Beyond them in the darkness near the walls she could distinguish the dignified faces of the ancient dead, her friends, her witnesses. Her eye returned to the centre of the flame and she saw within it with equanimity her own death.

Theodora kept her eye steadily on the flame. The silence filled her. The questions which had occupied her over the last two days fell away to be dealt with at the proper time. Now all that mattered was to find in the light of the candle silence, stillness, peace.

At eight o'clock the chimes of the cathedral clock drifted across suburb and marsh to the Hollow. One by one, as though reluctant to break the peace which silence had induced, the twelve began to stir. The legs of older members realigned themselves with their bodies none too nimbly. The lurcher bitch, who had been lying doggo in the shadow beside the boiler, rose, stretched, yawned and showed a lot of pink tongue and very white teeth. Stella went to the oven, Kevin stoked the boiler. Jewel carried bread to the table. Mr Bean collared Matt Rosen and talked about the wholesale price of timber. The conversation rose in volume, became general and cheerful. Goodwill was apparent.

They ate companionably. There was no sense of strain. No one patronised or chivvied or boasted. They were ordinary people who were glad to have been quiet with each other, who had done an honourable day's work, who had helped to grow at least some of the food they ate. Theodora, a connoisseur of the varieties of religious life, was reminded of some of the meals she had eaten in Africa with Africans. The Hollowmen were not, she noted, vegetarian. The casseroled meat was, if she was not mistaken, kid. The spinach, Jerusalem artichokes and potatoes came straight from the allotment. The cheese was light goat's and the dessert of nuts and apple was flavoured with their own honey. Fruits of the earth, she thought, and work of human hands.

'Yes,' said Stella in answer to Theodora's compliments, 'living here helps us to live slowly. We can attend to details and processes without being overwhelmed by them. We can afford to wait for things to germinate. But then we couldn't any of us live fast. We don't live in Nissen huts surrounded by goats and chickens because we could live in semis with garages and rockeries. We couldn't. We aren't normal people,'

Theodora looked at the plain steel dish holding the last of the dessert.

'Why did you leave the milk and honey offering in front of the Janus?' she asked on a sudden intuition.

Stella blushed. 'Partly gratitude. I felt him a kindred spirit. He won't fit into the present world either. And then, of course, we, Oliver and I, felt we need all the help we can get.'

'The office blocks?'

'Yes. The chapter seems set on letting them go ahead.'

Matt Rosen leaned across. 'Never say die. The *Examiner*'s doing us proud at the moment.' He turned to Oliver. 'It was a flattering profile of you in the "Life Style" series.'

Oliver smiled his beautiful smile. 'Late recognition. But of course it doesn't in the end matter if they move us on and we have to start again. The farm is there to show people that something can always come out of nothing.'

'I thought the attack on the chapter in today's edition was pertinent.' Gavin the Scot rolled his 'rs' and relished as only a presbyterian could the troubles of the English established episcopal Church.

'Do you know who writes them?' pursued Mrs Bean glancing at Canon Millhaven.

Erica extracted a kid bone fastidiously from her teeth and placed it on the side of her plate. 'You are right to infer inside knowledge, Mrs Bean, I'm sure.'

'You reckon someone done the dirt on them in the cathedral?' Jewel's gentle voice was full of genuine interest and entirely without malice.

'It's nice none of them seems to know what's to be done about the Janus, isn't it?' Miriam Rosen said.

Oliver grinned. 'Mark my words, before very long, chapter will be paying someone to take it away. I think they believe I put it there as a curse on them.'

'They don't seem to be picking up the dean's killer so quick,' was Kevin's contribution. He seemed pleased at the lack of police competence. But no one seemed to want to pursue the question of the dean's killer.

Finally they parted before midnight and Canon Millhaven drove Theodora back to the cathedral. ' "All sorts and conditions of men",' said Canon Millhaven in her elliptical way as they parked the car outside the Archgate.

'Action unites, belief divides,' said Theodora who could play this sort of game on and on. 'Work and food, the fundamentals of salvation,' she added.

'A terrible indictment of theology,' the

canon answered with genuine pleasure.

Together they strode across the turf of the close, two tall women in accord with each other, not needing to explain. As they approached the centre of the close the Janus reared up yet taller than Theodora remembered it. They paused for a moment as though in homage, then from round the scaffold base three small figures suddenly emerged. They were skipping, hopping, jumping, in an abandoned dance, hands waving above their heads in triumph or mockery.

'Ah,' said the Canon, 'there's hope for those young Riddables yet.'

CHAPTER NINE

MALIGN INFLUENCES

The fax was springy and slippery to the touch. In the cold morning air it smelt unfamiliarly chemical. It lay on the study table waiting for Theodora to attend to it. It must have come after she had set out for the Hollow yesterday evening for it had been waiting for her on her return. Too tired to look at it, she had retired to bed. At four she had risen, unable to sleep after the excitements of the day. She drew back the heavy curtains, pressed her nose to the cold glass and gazed at the double towers of the cathedral. She apprehended rather than saw the building rising out of its demented traffic and reflected on its clergy, dead and alive, jockeying and unamiable. She contemplated the Janus, charged, if the reactions of Stella and the Riddable children were anything to go by, with antique, ambiguous power. She thought of the Hollow with its ordinary ethic of work and its exceptional strength of silence and shared stillness. Here were three focuses of religious life. Were they complementary or opposed? Her heart, her loyalty, lay of course, with the cathedral but the other two were neglected at our peril, she thought.

What was it young Nick had said? 'No one loves anybody here.' That was true enough, but lack of love didn't usually lead to murder. Only in this case it had done. Where had the hatred sufficient to kill the dean come from?

She pulled the fax towards her and read what Geoffrey had written. 'Knight was a couple of years behind me at school and not in my house.' (Really, Theodora thought, these niceties of male acquaintance are not relevant.) 'Younger son of a North Riding baronet, Tristram Evelyn Knight. House colours for squash, school colours for sprint.' (Theodora clicked her tongue in impatience.) 'Left in his penultimate year under a cloud.' (Theodora thought how very much Geoffrey would have enjoyed having the opportunity to write that phrase.) 'There was some scandal about a boy who was later found with his wrists slashed. Joined RN as a rating. Later heard of at a refuge for alcoholics, St Crispin's in Wapping.'

Theodora stopped short. Surely she had heard the name earlier tonight. 'Come early,' Stella had said. 'Come before supper.' So Theodora had walked out along the straight marsh road under a low grey sky from which, as the light began to fade, warm drizzle had begun to fall. She had crossed the railway tracks and entered the Hollow. Stella was in one of the back sheds ladling out concentrates for the milking goats. The last of the school parties was wending its way to the coach down the gravel path which criss-crossed the sea of mud. Theodora and she had walked to the large goat pen with the lurcher bitch in attendance amiably chivvying the freely ranging hens. There they had fed the herd of black and white British Alpines and the odd long-haired Nubian. Theodora scratched their bony heads between their horns and smelt their goaty smell. Their hard yellow eyes had gazed insolently back at her.

'They're a good animal to have for city children to learn on,' Stella had said. 'There's no give in them. They don't care a toss. They can't be played with and they aren't toys. Children learn fairly quickly to be respectful.'

'Why do you think contact with animals makes us better as human beings would you say?' Theodora had inquired.

'Perspective. Shows us our place. Not ultimately the most important thing in the world.'

'Perhaps we should have one or two in the close,' Theodora mused.

'One of the young Riddables comes here every now and then. The middle boy, Tim, I think it is. He'd be a good goat herd,'

'"The chapter wouldn't like it",' Theodora quoted.

'Theirs the loss.'

There was a pause while they listened to the sound of goats dealing with concentrates. 'You asked about the dean,' Stella said hesitantly. 'I knew him, ten years ago just after I was married. Johnny, my husband, and I lived in Camden. I hadn't had Thomas, my son, then. I was looking for good works. There was a refuge for alcoholics in Wapping called St Crispin's. It abutted on to some church land. Two of the inmates were diagnosed as HIV positive. The trustees met the same week and the refuge was closed within twenty-four hours. They didn't know too much about AIDs at that time; it was early days. Anyway, they reacted like seventeenth-century mayors at the time of the plague. Everything was sealed up and fumigated. I don't know what on earth good they thought that would do. I managed to track down the chair of the trustees. It was Vincent Stream. At first he wouldn't see me. He said he'd nothing to say to the press. I pointed out that I wasn't press and that I'd worked at the refuge for three years as a volunteer. He clearly had no idea who worked there. I begged him to give the refuge a breathing space. There were these dozen men homeless and vulnerable. I asked him to delay or at least to rehouse. He practically bundled me out of his nice house. Probably thought I was infectious. Anyway he wouldn't rescind the order to close. We got up a head of steam locally but by that time the inmates were scattered. Later when the national press got hold of it he'd changed his tale to say that the arrangement for the closure of the house had been made a long time ago and that the inmates and helpers had been informed and the church needed the sale of the land to clear off past debts.'

Stella stopped. Theodora considered the tale. It rang true. A frightened, conventional and ignorant man had panicked. It wouldn't be the first time the church authorities had failed in charity and common sense. It certainly explained Stella's earlier remarks about the dean's lacking moral courage. There seemed nothing more to say on the topic. Theodora asked the obvious question. 'What happened to your own family?'

'I killed them.' Stella touched her scar. 'No, well, obviously not quite that. I was responsible for their death. I was driving them both in the car round the M25. I lost control.

We went through the central barrier. The ambulance couldn't get through because of the traffic. It was after that I came here. Erica Millhaven arranged it.'

That was what Stella had told her.

Theodora fingered Geoffrey's fax. So that was where she had met the name of St Crispin. Was there anything more than a coincidence in Tristram Knight having been at St Crispin's? Had he been an inmate or a helper? Was he there when the dean had turfed them out and closed the building down?

She looked at her watch. In an hour it would be time for the early Eucharist and then her meeting with Spruce to go through the dean's effects. She'd discuss it with him.

* * *

The mouse fixed her eye on the crumb of Stilton. 'Come on,' said Tim gently. 'Don't you like Stilton? I know it's a bit strong but it's all we had.' The mouse continued to turn her sharp profile towards him as though weighing up his trustworthiness. Tim was aware he was being judged. He withdrew his hand. At once the mouse flicked her tail, scuttled forward and hoovered up the cheese in one startling movement. Then she plopped down between the scaffold boards and disappeared from view. Tim let out his breath. He felt lightheaded with humility and gratitude. 'Oh, thank you so much,' he breathed.

High above him the bell began to toll for the early Eucharist. Very cautiously he shuffled backwards. The scaffold planks were rough and splintery to his hands and knees. The canvas flapped in the wind. He pulled a piece aside, grasped a scaffold pole, braced his foot against the earthen side of the hole and pulled himself up from the cavity from which the Janus had been recovered three days ago.

'Boo,' said his brother with delight.

Gratifyingly Tim jumped. 'You aren't supposed to be out alone,' he said to restore status.

'Well I'm not. I'm with you. What have you got in the cavern?'

It was not that Tim did not trust his brother, he told himself, but Ben didn't always seem to know what he was saying and to whom. At ten he himself had already developed the habit of keeping his own counsel.

'Nothing,' he said preparing to move off towards the Precentory.

'I know what you've got down there.' His brother galloped beside him. 'You've got the dean's murderer.'

Tim stopped. He was old enough to know you didn't joke about such matters. 'No I haven't. Don't be silly. Don't let Daddy hear you say things like that or you know what will happen.'

Ben ceased to walk beside his brother and

began to circle him, chopping his hand up and down. Then he began walking backwards and in consequence collided with Theodora who was walking forward. He picked himself up, was too embarrassed to make any apology and instead chose to continue the conversation with his brother.

'What if Daddy killed the dean,' Ben's high childish tone carried across the close. Theodora stopped and swung round.

Tim was appalled. 'Don't,' he said. 'Ben, don't.'

'Just testing,' Ben said clutching at a phrase he'd heard. Tim's tone frightened him. They stood in a row as though about to start some ritual. Ben looked up at Tim. Tim swung round to face Theodora, looking for help with something he could no longer cope with.

'Ben,' she said gently over the top of Tim's head. 'Have you learned to tell the time?'

Ben gazed at her for a moment, rather, Tim thought as he surveyed the two of them, as the mouse had looked at him a few moments ago. Then to Tim's surprise Ben burst into tears. 'It was the half that comes after twelve,' he said through his gulps.

'Yes,' said Theodora. 'I see. Did you make a mistake the first time you told us?'

Ben nodded, looking away from her. Then suddenly he turned his face towards her, his large grey eyes full of sincerity, and said, 'But I did see someone coming from the cathedral later. I mean after Daddy had come home.' He looked at Theodora as though inviting her to question him. She would have none of it and simply looked steadily back at him.

'I saw the man who does the digging, the archaeologist,' he paused, 'and before him there was a lady. I don't know which one. I couldn't see her very well.'

He smiled at Theodora with real pleasure.

* * *

Spruce turned in his pacing of the Deanery hall for the seventh time. He looked up at the face of the long-case clock. It ticked steadily back at him. It was indecent, Spruce felt, that the clock should tick on when its owner was dead. He looked round the hall. Its floor was of polished grey stone, the risers of the uncarpeted wooden stair were shallow, the panelling which covered all four walls was a foot taller than he was. Portraits of past deans marched up the staircase and round the gallery above. He was aware how much the building imposed its own style of living. Only certain sorts of movements, only certain ways of thinking were possible here. That's why buildings are important, he thought, they tell us how to behave. He thought of the cathedral. Then he thought of the dean. Had the dean felt this? Had he welcomed it or had he been daunted by it as Spruce was?

He was depressed by how little he knew of the dean forty-eight hours after his murder, how little progress he'd made towards solving the crime. All the information he'd been able to gain was on database, every statement, every address, even a graphic diagram of the scene of the murder. He was fast, he was accurate. He was known for both. But he had no pattern. The cathedral, the Janus, the Hollow, how did they relate to each other and to the murder of, presumably, a religious man, anyway a professional churchman?

The police still had no certain timetable of his movements prior to his death. No weapon had been found, no motive had come to light. None of the suspects looked all that suspicious. He'd started the day with a testing twenty minutes with his superintendent who'd admitted in a fatherly way that he'd been leant on by his chief constable. The bishop suffragan had inquired, Canon Riddable had complained, the diocesan secretary had wanted to know, the chancellor (whatever that was) of the diocese had suggested. In a word the diocesan establishment had united to make matters as difficult and unpleasant as possible for him and his men. They'd none of them been able to add to the sum of knowledge about the crime: clerical convenience and importance appeared to be their first and only consideration.

The more he contemplated these cathedral

clergy the less he understood them, their attitudes and presuppositions seemed to belong to another world. What did they think they were doing? He compared them with his own father who had been a methodist lay preacher all his working life. When he wasn't organising the local union and raising funds for the Wesleyan old people's home, he'd dug his allotment, all of which his son still thought admirable activities. Spruce's eye caught that of a seventeenth-century dean who had been painted standing beside a Deanery window with a view of the double-towered cathedral in the background. In the portrait the dean's hand rested on a skull. That's more like it, Spruce said to himself. That's more of the proper religious attitude. That's what they should be doing for us, for themselves, nowadays, reminding us of death. Nothing like a good memento mori.

'I'm sorry to keep you waiting,' said Theodora as she pushed the Deanery door closed behind her. 'I've just met the Riddable children.'

'The question is,' she concluded when she had shared her information with Spruce, 'can we trust young Riddable this time about the timing of his father's movements and his observation of these two other people, presumably Fresh and a woman?'

Spruce nodded. 'The little tyke. What did he think he was doing first time round?'

'Shopping his father for murder.'

'Not a pretty boy.'

'True enough,' said Spruce recollecting. 'How would you say that left us as regards Riddable as a suspect?'

'If we can rely on Ben for the timing it means that he couldn't have done it. If we can't rely on Ben then he might have done it. And if we believe Ivan Markewicz Riddable had a motive.'

'What exactly did your friend Markewicz say?' Spruce inquired.

'He told me Riddable had asked him to publish this thing he'd written. Markewicz didn't think it was up to scratch but didn't quite like to say so off his own bat. So he sent it to the dean and asked him what he thought. The dean was quite eloquent, according to Ivan, on how bad it was. So Ivan felt strong enough to refuse the article and told Riddable what the dean had said.'

Spruce grinned. 'Was that tactful, or usual even?'

'Neither, but I gather he didn't care for Riddable who exercised his usual charm of manner and managed to be both arrogant and importunate.He told Ivan three times that he was a residentiary canon and seemed to suppose this guaranteed the quality of his writing.'

'The point is, would Riddable's being angry at the dean about the article be a motive for murder?' Spruce sounded doubtful.

Theodora shook her head. 'Only if one assumes a quarrel. I can imagine Riddable killing someone in anger by accident. I can't imagine him cutting a man's throat and lugging him thirty yards to deposit him in front of the Janus.'

Spruce sighed. 'If it weren't clergy, I'd pull him down the station and lean on him. But what with the superintendent and the chief constable and uncle Tom Cobbleigh and all, I do really need more than a scholar's tiff and a seven-year-old liar's fantasies to go on.'

Theodora sysmpathised. 'What about the alternatives? The archaeologist Ben Riddable mentioned.'

'I'll have another go at Fresh,' said Spruce. 'In his statement of yesterday, he said he'd left the close about eight-thirty in the evening and gone to see a bee-keeper at Quecourt. He got back to the Hollow about midnight. The bee-keeping bit was right enough. The Hollow I'm not so sure about. The woman, what's her name, Parish, Stella Parish, had thought she'd heard Fresh come in but wasn't sure.'

Theodora marked the interesting fact that she'd supposed that Stella and Oliver shared a bed and if Spruce's statement was right, they didn't. How very careful one did have to be.

Theodora prowled round the hall, pacing the path that Spruce had taken a moment or two previously. Spruce squatted on the bottom step of the stairs. 'What about the woman figure Ben says he saw in addition to Fresh, if it was Fresh? Would that be Canon Millhaven?'

'There aren't many other women in the close. Mrs Riddable says she was tucked up in bed.'

'What's the order of appearance then if we trust Ben?'

Spruce ticked it off on his fingers. 'The party ends *circa* midnight and the Riddables come home together across the close. That's according to the Riddable daughter. Then Canon Riddable goes back to tell the dean the services are too long. He returns according to Ben at half past twelve. Then also according to the Riddable daughter, the dean comes out of the Deanery and heads towards the cathedral, time, soon after the return of her father, say twelve-forty. After that Ben, if he's telling the truth, sees the dean come out of the cathedral followed by, presumably, Fresh and an unknown woman, possibly Canon Millhaven.'

'Time?'

'Stroke of one?'

'Too many ones,' said Theodora.

'There's the one for twelve-thirty, the one for one and the one for one-thirty.' Spruce recited like an incantation. 'The one for one-thirty is too late because the dean's watch tells us he was dead by ten past one. The one for twelve-thirty is too early, if we believe the Riddables that they were all back in the Precentory by then. What we're looking for is people who were about and murderously inclined at one a.m. Fresh and Millhaven perhaps.'

Theodora contemplated the idea of either of those killing the dean and thought how very much she did not want it to be the case. She thought of Geoffrey's information about Tristram Knight which she had not yet shared with Spruce.

'Would it be a good idea,' Theodora said hesitantly, 'to check with the vergers again, Knight and Nick Squires to see if they noticed anyone else lingering from the party?'

Spruce recognised her feelings. 'Yes. Meanwhile I wondered if you could bear to go through the dean's effects with me. In particular we got some stuff out of his safe which I'd like your views on. It's time we had a motive.'

'What have you got on the dean's background?' Theodora inquired as they mounted the stairs.

'Precious little. His parents are dead. He was an only child. His executors are his bank. He's got a cousin in Canada who gets his cash, about eight thousand. His college gets his books. The furniture here, I gather belonged to the old dean who left it to the Diocesan Board of Finance on the understanding it should stay *in situ*.'

Theodora was amused. 'Perhaps the old dean was worldly enough to realise his successors might not have large private incomes and affluent inheritances. You need such big pieces to fill rooms this size.'

Two floors up they came to rest in the dean's bedroom. There was nothing in it, nothing, that is to say, to reveal the character of the man. There was a narrow single bed, a table which held the English Missal and an Office Book with the purple marker for Ash Wednesday in place. Over the bed was a small crucifix.

Theodora looked round with embarrassment. 'It is the ultimate in voyeurism, judging a man by his effects.'

'By their fruits ye shall know them,' said Spruce who perhaps felt her scruples as a criticism of his own trade.

'It's not at all the same thing,' Theodora snapped. 'Would you care to be judged by your waistcoats?'

'Talking of clothes,' said Spruce equably, 'there's nothing in his wardrobe except clerical dress. Would you say that was usual?'

It was on the tip of Theodora's tongue to say that she wasn't in the habit of peering into the closets of celibate priests. Did the man not realise there were limits to her knowledge of clerical matters? 'It does seem a bit extreme,' she admitted cautiously.

Her eye swept the room. There was nothing personal in it, nothing to link him to anything except the church. Was this bareness the austerity of a disciplined life, or had he feared just such an intrusion as this and determined that there should be no evidence to convict him? But convict him of what, Theodora wondered. Then she recalled Stella's anecdote about the St Crispin's refuge and her previous remark: 'He lacks moral courage.' Certainly he lacked the courage to make any personal display. He was content to live amongst another man's inherited furniture and had on his own account wanted to add practically nothing. She took in the shelf above the wash handbasin in the corner of the room. Shaving brush and soap, toothbrush and powder and hand soap were neatly arranged. Surely he must have been the last man in England to use coal tar soap.

In the study on the ground floor there was the same feeling of a life lived out of very little. The books were solid reference texts, Hastings, Cross, a selection from Migne, an anthology of passages from modern Christian Catholic theologians. It was a collection for someone who wanted to *show* knowledge rather than to explore or possess it.

Spruce busied himself with keys to open the old-fashioned safe in the far corner of the room. Theodora wandered about trying to recall how the room had looked when she had glanced in on the night of the party. Her eye was caught by a box file balanced on the bookcase shelf beneath a gap from which it had clearly been taken. Idly she pressed the spring catch and glanced at the contents. It was filled with letters and press cuttings. Both stretched back over thirty years. The letters seemed to be all congratulatory. 'Vincent, thank you for a really excellent sermon, packed with meat in your usual style', read one card bearing the address of a lately deceased Bishop of London. 'Dear Father, it was such a comfort to have you take Jeremy's funeral,' read another. Mixed in were press reports of his public appearances, the odd gossip columnist mention, a thoughtful review of a reissue of his early anthology of spiritual advice 'Saving Souls' from the *Church Times*. The last cutting laid on top of the pile was the *Bow Examiner*'s report of his installation. Was this his one concession to personality?

Theodora was about to replace the file in its place, when her eye was caught by a cutting yellower and older than the ones which surrounded it. The headline leaped at her. 'St Crispin's Refuge: Volunteer Helper Speaks Out' ran the headline. It went on, 'Stella Parish, 28, a volunteer helper for three years at St Crispin's by Wapping Steps roundly condemned the church authorities for closing the Refuge yesterday. "There's no danger," she told our reporter on the steps of the refuge "and it's made half a dozen very vulnerable men homeless." We contacted one of the inmates, Tristram Knight, a former RN gunner ...'. Theodora stopped. She turned to Spruce who was having difficulty with the lock of the safe. Swiftly she scanned the rest of the brief report. Then she closed the file and replaced it.

'You can read a balance sheet I take it,' Spruce said as he placed the gleanings from the safe on the dean's desk.

'Can you look at this lot and from your experience of how "Friends of the Cathedral" funds work, let me know what you think?'

'The only experience I've had of cathedral finances was as a very junior deacon attached to the cathedral in Nairobi.'

'Well, see what you make of this,' Spruce pressed.

Theodora found his faith in her knowledge of clerical matters, whether of the sartorial customs of Anglo-Catholic clergy or of the financial practices of cathedrals, rather touching. She took a pencil and sheet of paper from the immaculate pad on the dean's desk and set to work.

Half an hour later she leaned back in the chair. 'I suppose you want me to say that Archdeacon Gold is either very slipshod or downright dishonest?'

Spruce smiled with relief. 'I thought I'd get your impression before we set an accountant on. Now, would the dean have known that Gold was fiddling the books, do you suppose?'

'It would be unusual for these things,' she

indicated the sheets of figures, 'to be in the dean's private safe unless he was scrutinising them. They would more usually be kept in the cathedral office.'

Spruce smiled contentedly. 'Would the dean have revealed that knowledge, if he had it, to Gold?'

Theodora tapped her pencil on the paper pad. 'Presumably you haven't questioned Gold?'

Spruce shook his head. 'Not about any previous conversation he might have had with the dean prior to the party. His statement about his movements on the night of the murder after the party, you may remember, claimed he spent the night at Brian Brace's, the chairman of the County Council Finance Committee. However, in the light of this we'll have another go at him and see if we can crack it. I'd like to get somebody charged with something out of all this even if it's only fraud.'

Theodora smiled at him pityingly. 'You won't manage that,' she said confidently. 'The church will never press charges. He wouldn't be allowed to go on as an archdeacon, but he'd not be sent for trial.'

Spruce was scandalised. 'But it's dishonest.'

'Maybe, but the Christian tradition stemming from St Paul advises no recourse to pagan law courts to settle disputes between Christians. This is nowadays transmuted into "no dirty linen in public".'

'The clergy have got to be seen to be morally irreproachable even if they're not.'

'A less charitable way of putting it,' said Theodora serenely. 'I'd concentrate on the murder. Could the man who came out of the cathedral after the dean on the night of the murder be Gold?'

'I thought young Riddable said it was Fresh or anyway the man who dug up the Janus?'

'But is he reliable?'

Spruce sucked his teeth in irritation. 'I'm going to have to get a WPC and go over that young man, however much I don't want to.'

'You mean you're afraid of what his father might do to him?'

'I could get his mother to be with him. Would you think that might make it easier for him?'

Theodora considered what she knew and what she felt about Mrs Riddable. 'She's deeply manipulative, in my view. So it would depend on what game she was playing with whom as to whether she protected her son.'

'God rot the clergy,' Spruce burst out in irritation.

'They can be aggravating,' Theodora agreed without rancour as she rose from her chair at the dean's desk and prepared to depart. 'By the way, when I came to the party on Tuesday night, I seem to remember I saw a very large desk diary or day book open on this desk. You haven't found it, I suppose.'

'No,' said Spruce morosely. 'We haven't.'

CHAPTER TEN

SERVANTS' QUARTERS

First there was the sound of music. Those who had attended the dean's installation might have recognised Bow Youth Silver Band. Nick pressed the button on the machine and there was a whirring sound. 'If we do not have God in our hearts, then we have nothing in our hearts,' said the light, clipped tone of the late dean as he ended his sermon. Nick's long finger hovered over the control button as the sounds continued. He pressed the fast forward then the playback button. This time there was a woman's voice and the dean's answering it. Both voices were angry. There were a couple of clicks and then silence.

Nick sat back on his heels. The vestry was empty. The early afternoon light seeped through the one high round window. He wondered what to do. The idea of destroying evidence went against the whole of his scholarly instinct. In a shaky world where few cared for truth and there wasn't, he'd found, much to hang on to, he saw the historian's task as one not merely of seeking out information but also guarding it, preserving and making it accessible. If he had a temperamental weakness he recognised that it lay in his delight in making patterns out of bits and pieces of information. A rearrangement of a couple of potsherds, a bit of broken epigraphy and a disputed reference to a solar eclipse in Thucydides and the whole of pre-Christian chronology could come tumbling down. He loved the fragility of such scholarly constructs. But when it came to a matter which touched him deeply he was surprised to find how reluctant he was to fit the pieces together.

There was the question of the Church or more particularly Bow St Aelfric cathedral. He knew very well that in a sense the cathedral had made him. It had been his first and his fullest intimation of a world alternative to the one his father inhabited up on the Peterborough bypass. He remembered the first time he'd set eyes on the building. He must have been about eight. It had been soon after his mother's death. His father had brought him down to the city and they'd walked into the close through the Archgate one perfect June evening. The silence closed in on them, the double towers rose up one behind the other with the sun catching the west end. The choir had been walking across from the school to sing Evensong. He'd taken it all in, beauty, order, antiquity, and decided that that was how he'd live. And so, so far, it had proved. Their next-door neighbour had given him singing lessons.

He'd got a choral scholarship, passed effortlessly through the choir school and later the adjacent grammar school. The cathedral gave him a complete world, totally satisfying to both sense and intellect. His concentration had been strengthened by the musical discipline, his senses daily satisfied by the textures and colours of an inexhaustible building. That building and the life within it had steadied and anchored his sensitivities which might otherwise have destroyed him.

He felt no call to the priesthood. His notion of God was that He was undoubtedly there, but might not be as concerned with men as men thought He was. Perhaps He was even morally neutral, not necessarily what we think Him to be. We could have got Him wrong, Nick the historian began to feel, as he read his history and observed his world. Certainly the antics of those who professed to know Him best engendered no confidence. Nevertheless, Nick's love, his real gratitude, for the place, the institution and what it stood for, made him hesitate now to put it in jeopardy. He looked at the tape machine. All that he was most attached to seemed threatened by it. But it was evidence.

Far above him he heard the door into the vestry passage from the cathedral bang shut. Swiftly he ejected the tape and stuffed it into a carton, then, together with the large leather-bound volume, he wrapped it in his pullover and crammed them into his holdall. The door swung open and Tristram stood on the threshold. Nick's face cleared into a beautiful smile. 'I thought Dennis was doing Evensong.'

'He wants a change. I'll do Evensong. Can you do Eucharist tomorrow?'

'Fine. How about Compline?'

'Cancelled.'

'You can't, can you, on your own authority?'

'Not mine, the chapter's. Or at least Canon Riddable's I suspect.'

'Ho, ho. A return to the lax old ways. Now the dean's dead we shall be racing through an abbreviated form of the Eucharist and calling it a day. What has Riddable got against religion would you say?'

'I think it makes him feel uneasy. Confronts him with realities he'd rather not acknowledge.'

'Such as?'

'Death,' said Tristram grimly. 'And repentance perhaps.'

* * *

Mrs Perfect in the diocesan office pressed 'print' and watched the A 11 continuous begin to roll from the machine. She reached into her drawer, brought out a tube of Polos and refreshed herself after her labours. The office had been bedlam all day, well, all week really, if you came to think of it. Thank God for Friday.

She sometimes wondered why she worked for the church. They paid badly, the holidays were mean, they didn't provide even luncheon vouchers. The amount of work was formidable since by any normal standards they were understaffed. The cathedral clergy themselves were mostly disorganised, peremptory and, Mrs Perfect, a regular *Times* Crossword woman, reflected, poor spellers. What kept her in place, she had to admit, was pity. She felt a surge of protectiveness whenever one or other of them displayed their failings. If she could, she'd have liked to take them back home with her, enclose them in proper family affection and send them out again into the world new made over, to do better. Failing that, she corrected their spelling and syntax and was unfailingly kind to them all.

Towards their office equipment, however, Mrs Perfect had no such generous feeling. She had worked for Plessey in their smart warehouse beyond the Hollow and knew what good equipment was. The cathedral's stuff was awful. They were always buying models of things which had just gone out of production and which didn't fit with each other. They had four different sorts of typeface, five if you counted that thing from the verger's office. Her eye swung towards the ancient Remington which stood beside the other three office machines. The young man from Autotype was working his way along them. He looked about twelve and a half and had an earring in his left ear. Still, he seemed to know what he was doing.

She looked out of the window and rubbed it with her sleeve to get a clearer view of the close. The rain which had made shopping in the lunch hour such a burden had ceased and pale spring sun warmed the stone. It was only her fancy, of course, but it seemed to her that day by day, every day since its discovery, the Janus had risen a little bit higher out of its vault. It stood now presiding over the close. It seemed not at all abashed by its Christian surroundings. It held court at all hours of the day to a changing group of admirers. Some of them stayed for long periods. Yesterday, Sir Lionel Dunch had brought a party of archaeologists and antiquarians round. He had stood with his foot on the plinth and lectured them. School parties were frequent, there were a couple of watercolourists and small compact posses of Japanese. Local and national TV crews had come and gone.

The chapter, what remained of it, she knew were beginning to hate him. They were much more concerned about the Janus than they were about finding the dean's murderer. Even now Canon Riddable and Archdeacon Gold were discussing what to do about him. The door between her office and the archdeacon's was imperfectly closed. Every now and again when the exchange got heated their remarks became audible.

'If we let Dunch have it,' said the archdeacon, 'we shan't get a penny for it.'

'So what?' Riddable's hectoring tone was easier to hear than the archdeacon's.

They sounded like a couple of middle managers at Plessey, Mrs Perfect decided. In a crisis, neither of them had much in the way of language or moral discernment to see them through.

'We've simply got to get the odd bob together.' The archdeacon sounded desperate.

He was carrying on as though it was his personal fortune which was at stake. As though he might have to sell the XJ, Mrs Perfect thought. And how would that look to all those financial politicians like Brian Brace, whom he so much admired?

'The important thing is to get it off the premises,' Riddable was pressing on. 'Do you realise what it's doing?'

'How do you mean?'

'It's attracting worship.'

'What?'

'I found a couple of little cards stuck on it this morning asking for its help.'

'What sort of help?' The archdeacon was stung to curiosity.

Mrs Perfect could hear Canon Riddable flushing. 'In sexual matters,' he mumbled with distaste.

'Pretty traditional,' the archdeacon replied liberally. 'I seem to remember from Pompeii . . .'

'I don't care a damn about Pompeii. This is England. I want it out. Do you understand?' Mrs Perfect heard the sound of a table being slapped. Riddable was at it again. She sensed the frustration lying at the heart of his ill-conditioned nature.

'Well, I suppose we could get it out of the close. But I don't want to pay for storage.'

'Get it out,' Riddable paused between each word.

'All right, all right. I'll have a word with Dunch or Fresh and see if they can help.'

'You do that,' Riddable's tone was suddenly comradely. The change was breathtaking. 'I'm sure I can leave it in your very capable hands, Archie.' Anyone would have thought he was the senior of the two. There was a scraping of chairs. Mrs Perfect moved from the window back to her desk. She picked up the phone and gazed at the ceiling as Riddable came out and swept towards the door.

'Miss Braithwaite? Mrs Perfect here, cathedral office. I have two messages for you. A Mr,' she looked at the note, 'Markewicz rang and said the date you wanted was the tenth. That's right. And the second message . . . Canon Millhaven would be glad if you could call on her at six-thirty today. Oh and Miss Braithwaite, there's a parcel come for you.

Yes. Yes of course I'll do that. We close at five-thirty but I can leave it on the table in the outer office for you if you like.'

*　　*　　*

Spruce ate the last of his luncheon kebab and dried his hands finger by finger on a very clean white handkerchief. Mules belied his tranquil demeanour by making a series of racing changes to circumvent the dawdling afternoon traffic on the outskirts of Bow. They hit the roadworks and slowed down again.

'When I was a boy, they never carried on like this. There were no building sites and the roads stayed down.'

Mules looked at him as though at a fractious child. 'It'll pass, sir, never you worry.'

Spruce began to sort out his thoughts. First there was the matter of motive. The difficulty was that different contexts produce different sorts of motives. Gamblers, drug traffickers and fraudulent accountants were stirred to kill by different things. What would move the clergy to commit murder?

Spruce glanced at Mules's lugubrious profile. 'What would you commit murder for, Mules? Money, reputation, revenge?'

'I might have a go for revenge,' Mules ventured. 'People ought to pay their debts.'

'But not money?'

'That'd just be greedy, wouldn't it, sir? Not a

justifiable act.'

'So you think the dean died for a justifiable reason?'

'He was laid out very carefully, wasn't he. So whoever killed him may have thought he was justified. Less a murder, more an execution.'

'How about Archdeacon Gold? It looks as though he's had a hand in the till.' Spruce tried it out on his sergeant by way of experiment.

'He's buddy-buddy with the Council, both finance and planning. Which, of course, he needs to be if he's going to get the Hollow development through.'

'He's also got an expensive taste in cars.'

'An XJ and a little MG tourer. He's also got a power boat up the coast at Narborough.' Mules gestured with his right hand towards the rain-soaked horizon.

Spruce looked at his sergeant with admiration. 'How come you know that?'

'I have dabbled in that line myself,' Mules was modest.

'Do we know whether the dean knew about the archdeacon's activities with the finances?'

'We can't be sure, but the evidence was stashed in his safe as though for use.'

'Would Gold kill to stop it being revealed that he was a thief?'

Spruce shook his head. 'Not a matter of public revelation but as archdeacon he stood to lose a heck of a lot. Miss Braithwaite says the Church wouldn't prosecute but they'd certainly remove him. He'd not be employable as an archdeacon.'

'A small country living?' Mules accelerated with pleasure at the thought.

'He'd feel the change from being fêted by the local politicians. Have to sell the XJ maybe. The question is,' Spruce pressed on, 'could he have done it in the time?'

'I checked the timing with him again. He went back to Brace's flat at the far end of Watergate. That's ten minutes walking, five by car, from the cathedral. They all went by car. Each in his own.'

'Where do they start from exactly? The cars weren't taken into the close, as I understand it.'

'There's no parking of anything in the close. The vergers bring their bicycles in but they shouldn't and they tend to conceal them in the choir school basement, according to Nick Squires. On the night of the murder all the guests had to leave their cars in the magistrates' court car park to the north of the cathedral. The clergy regularly have places reserved for them there. It's no distance. Brace says they were at his flat by twelve-ten. They drank whisky till about twelve-thirty. Then Gold said he'd better not drive so Brace invited him to stay the night. Gold rang his wife to let her know. She agreed he rang about ten to one.'

'Then what?' Spruce turned to look at his colleague's profile as he went smoothly through the gears and marshalled his facts.

'Brace says he and Gold turned in. Brace admits that Gold could have got out of the flat at any time and come back in without anyone noticing. There are no staff and it would only be a matter of leaving the door on the latch. But on the other hand he says he heard nothing and Gold says he slept straightaway. My impression was that Brace was tight and he was implying that Gold was too.'

'So unless Gold was faking and unless he was a very smart runner, he'd have all on to slip out of Brace's and sprint down to the cathedral to kill the dean by ten past one.'

'He is a runner, actually. I've seen him jogging.'

'But look,' Spruce said reasonably, 'the dean was killed just outside the cathedral. How would the archdeacon know he was going over to the cathedral at that time? I mean for all he knew he might have had to break into the Deanery.'

'He might have made an appointment with the dean earlier in the evening.' Mules was equally reasonable.

' "Meet me behind the cathedral, Dean, at one p.m. after your party and I'll kill you," doesn't sound convincing, does it?'

'No,' Mules admitted, 'but it's not impossible. However,' he paused for effect and to avoid a clutch of JCBs doing a square dance round the earth works, 'however, the archdeacon did add one further bit of information second time round. He says he saw Fresh outside the cathedral gate as he was leaving.'

'Fresh, eh? Was he sure?'

'Pretty sure.'

'So what was Fresh doing outside the Archgate at midnight? And why did he not mention it in his first statement to us? He hasn't got a key to the close gate has he?'

'Not so far as anyone knows.'

'Right. We'll press him on that as well as on the other thing. Now, how about the weapon?'

'Nothing,' Mules was regretful.

'It's bloody annoying we haven't found one. That's another thing that makes me feel this killing was planned.' Spruce ruminated. By now the car had entered the road which ran beside the railway track skirting the Hollow. 'Most murderers do tend to want to get rid as soon as possible. Only a very deliberate murderer takes elaborate pains to conceal the weapon.'

'What did Doctor Gibbon say it might have been?'

'Anything from a lino cutter to a razor.'

'We could get a warrant and search the archdeacon's dustbin?' Mules didn't sound that keen.

'Forget it. I've already had the superintendent telling me that the chief constable told him about my methods. We'd need much more to go on than the archdeacon's sprinting ability and an unproven capacity for living beyond his means.' But even as he said this Spruce knew that if it had been any other context, if, that is to say, they hadn't been clergymen, he'd have had a search warrant and been over the archdeacon's stuff long ago.

'How about Riddable?' Mules asked since they were clearly going through the main suspects.

Spruce sighed. 'I'm tempted to dismiss him as just a buffoon. But he's certainly violent in language if nothing else, and Miss Braithwaite says Nick Squires told her he used to beat up boys when he taught in the school.'

'Some deserve it,' said Mules stoically. 'And it's a long haul from disciplining schoolboys to cutting your dean's throat.'

'He has a motive.'

'That article business you told me about, trying to publish something he hadn't written, wasn't it? What would he lose if the dean did know about it?'

'Face.'

'To a man of Riddable's type,' Spruce said, 'that's probably the most important thing in life. We come back to my initial point about different contexts bringing out different motives.'

'So what do you make of the timing for him?'

'He left the dean soon after midnight and walked his wife across the close. Ten minutes later he went back across the close to see the dean. You heard what he said about wanting to put him right on service times.'

Mules turned his unbelieving face towards Spruce, momentarily abandoning his careful circumnavigation of the potholes.

'Yes, well. We neither of us believed him at the time and it doesn't gain anything in the retelling, I grant you.'

'So what *did* he go to see the dean about?'

'His article?'

'It must have been pressing to slip back at that time. However, let's suppose it was the article. Why should it suddenly become pressing?'

'May be,' Spruce conjectured, 'he needed to be in print and the dean's veto prevented that.'

'It's too complicated for me.' Mules complained.

'No, look, don't lose heart,' Spruce was animated. 'Riddable admits he returned to the Deanery. Wouldn't those two servants, vergers, Nick and the Knight fellow, still have been there? Nick Squires says he left at twelve-fifteen and Knight says he went off at twelve-thirty. Whether they saw Riddable will depend on how public he made his appearance. Presumably they'd both have been in the kitchen basement.'

Mules nodded. 'They might have heard something of the dean—Riddable conversation. Riddable isn't one to keep his voice down.'

'We'll check it,' said Spruce, 'the minute we've finished at the Hollow. Now what happened next? Say they quarrelled about the article for whatever reason. His son, the little one, now says he went back to the Precentory on the stroke of twelve-thirty. The girl, his daughter then saw the dean go from the Deanery via the Janus to the cathedral. The boy then says he saw the dean come out again and that a man and a woman were about in the close at the same time.'

'Proper little spy. The lad.'

'And not too reliable. Doesn't care for his dad.'

'Join the crowd.' Mules permitted himself a grin, switched the indicator left and turned for the Hollow.

'Let's take him and his sister at their face value. The canon gets back to the Precentory at twelve-thirty at which point the dean's still alive. Why did he go to the cathedral at that time of night and who are the man and the woman following him as he comes out?'

'The boy said "the archaeologist who dug up the Janus," something like that.'

'So you reckon it was Fresh? That means there are two witnesses to Fresh being in the area at about the right time.'

'And the woman?'

'Millhaven? Or Fresh's woman? Parish. Mrs Stella Parish.'

The car swung through the Hollow's gates, slowed to a crawl to let a couple of Khaki Campbells sway across the track, and pulled up in front of the Nissen hut.

The first thing which struck Spruce about Fresh's room was that it contained a dozen possible murder weapons. There were saddlers' knives, carpenters' knives, all neat and clean and glittering with freshly sharpened edges.

'Oliver's out with Kevin, Inspector. They're doing the fences by the cutting. He'll be in for tea in ten minutes. I expect you'll want to wait. Perhaps you'd care for some tea?'

Mrs Parish seemed to Spruce to be perfectly composed. She fondled the ears of the lurcher bitch and included them all in her hospitality.

'Could you spare us a moment first, Mrs Parish? It would help us if we could get one or two things absolutely straight.'

'I've nothing really to add to what I told your sergeant before.' However she drew up chairs for them all near the boiler in the centre of the room.

'The night the dean was killed. You said in your statement, Mr Fresh came back from Quecourt at about one-thirty. How does he travel? Has he got a car?'

'He goes everywhere by bike. He feels cars aren't environmentally friendly.' She paused briefly then went on. 'I don't drive myself now. Oliver came back from the cathedral at about nine. He'd stayed to put the Janus to bed, as he put it. I think he said something about expecting Dunch, Sir Lionel Dunch, the archaeologist, to meet him at the Janus, but he hadn't done so. Dunch was going to the dean's party. Oliver, of course, was not. When he got back he had a meal and then went straight out to Quecourt to see Mr Moulsham about queens for next year. Bees. Mr Moulsham is a national authority. Perhaps you know him?'

Spruce regretted he didn't have that pleasure but Sergeant Mules had taken his statement.

'Couldn't he have rung Moulsham?' Spruce inquired.

'We aren't on the phone here, Inspector.'

Spruce evinced astonishment. 'But your many visitors?'

'If they want to come they must take the trouble to make a reconnaissance. We aren't a raree-show. We have a way of life to offer. They must come and sample it.'

'Then they too can get wet to the skin.' Fresh said stamping through the door from the kitchen part of the hut. 'Good afternoon to you both.' His large satyr smile took them all in. It held nothing, Spruce thought, except excellent health, a quiet conscience and good will. Fresh filled the room with his presence. He continued taking off waterproofs and stepping out of boots. Everything had a place. Stella had not moved at his entry. If anything she relaxed and contemplated him as a delighted spectator.

The lurcher wove in and out of his legs trying her best to unbalance him.

A lesser man than Spruce would have asked to see Fresh on his own. But in Spruce's experience the more relaxed people were, the less they feared you, the more they were going to tell you. It wasn't a policy officially approved amongst the senior members of the force but it had served Spruce well in the past. If Stella wanted to stay while he went over the ground again then he wasn't going to make a fuss.

'How well did you know the late dean, Mr Fresh?' Spruce's tone was relaxed, interested, conversational. They could have been discussing a mutual acquaintance of whom they both regretted the passing.

'I first met him when he came down about six weeks ago, before his installation. He was walking round the cathedral. Of course deans do tend to feel they own cathedrals. Responsibility without ownership is a difficult notion for them to grasp. It's bound up with power. Knowing that you alone know what is best for people is corrupting. Sometimes you can pass it off as vision. Other times it looks like coercion or hubris. You know about hubris, Inspector?'

'You meet a lot of it in the criminal world.' Spruce was not at all put out. 'How did hubris take Dean Stream?'

'He wanted to reorder the building without

any regard for its age or purpose. Modern glass doors at the west end are not what the fourteenth-century masons who put up that porch had in mind. It would have done nothing to enhance the feeling you should get as you enter the shadow of the cathedral. It ought to feel like birth, the beginning of a journey. Entering a cathedral is a pilgrimage from the setting sun in the west to the rising sun in the east, from dark to light, from death to birth. It's not like, it ought not to be like, entering any other building.'

'Did he take your point?'

Fresh grinned. 'Not in the least. His understanding was clouded by *his* importance and *my* unimportance. He did not allow my words to rest in his mind for a single moment.'

Spruce caught a glimpse of what Fresh might have been like in an earlier age: a Fox or a Bunyan trying to get the established church to listen to the people instead of telling them all the time. He would not have been surprised if Fresh had quoted scripture.

'The eyes of the blind shall be opened and the ears of the deaf shall hear. But only at the end of time, Inspector.' Spruce nodded at Fresh's words.

'Would what the dean wanted to do have evoked strong feeling amongst the other members of the chapter, Mr Fresh?'

'Ah well, that I couldn't say. I'm not privy to their counsels. I doubt if anyone would kill for aesthetic reasons nowadays, in our society, would you say, Inspector?' Fresh might have been laughing at him, Spruce couldn't tell.

'Someone did kill the dean. Would you have any ideas who might want to do that?'

Fresh glanced at Stella. 'Perhaps it was a voice from his past. Have you thought of that?'

Spruce who was aware how very little of any use the police had been able to find out about the dean's dull past was rather caught by this.

'Do you know anything of his past, Mr Fresh?'

'I? No, not I.'

'What about his plans for the future?' Spruce sharpened the offensive. 'I understand the chapter were keen to use this land to build offices on. What are your feelings about that?'

'Sufficient unto the day.'

'Meaning?'

'If he wants this land to put up offices that no one needs to finance his wrecking of the cathedral, we shall not make it easy for him but in the end, we know the world. The law is on his side. We shall move on and start again. That is precisely our strength. That is precisely what we have to offer the world. Like plants through cracks in concrete we shall shoot up again.'

Spruce reckoned he'd got what he wanted. There was ample evidence of motive for killing if he ever needed to prove it. He felt able to move on.

'The night of the murder, Shrove Tuesday.

You went to Quecourt to see about bees after supper, about nine p.m.'

'Yes.'

'Then what?'

'In the end I returned to sleep here.'

'In the end?'

'That's what I said.'

'You were seen outside the Archgate at about midnight that night.'

'Yes. That's possible.'

'You didn't mention it in your previous statement.'

'I didn't want to raise your hopes, Inspector. I had nothing so far as I know to do with the murder of the dean.'

'What were you doing there?'

'I went back to see to Janus.'

Spruce noticed the lack of the definite article. The man was speaking of the statue as though it were a person.

'How do you mean "see to" him, it?'

'The temperature was dropping. It had been wet. I feared for the action of the water on the newly exposed metal. I also wanted to see Sir Lionel Dunch to talk about Janus's future.'

'Did you see Sir Lionel?'

'No. He'd gone. The young verger, Nick Squires, who was keeping the gate, told me the bishop suffragan had given him a lift back to Quecourt. I think everyone had gone by that time. Nick was twirling his keys on his ring in a meaningful manner.'

'So what did you do?'

'I tried to get Nick to let me in to see to Janus. He played with the idea but in the end proved incorruptible. He seemed to think it was late and he'd have to let me out again, which would be inconvenient. He was courteous but regretful. So I took up my bike and came home. I arrived back about twelve-thirty.' He looked at Stella who nodded.

'The cathedral clock had just struck,' she offered.

'Struck once?' Spruce inquired wearily.

'That's right.'

'How long does it take to get from the cathedral to the Hollow?'

'By bike? It depends on the traffic but at that time of night and at my pace, half an hour.'

There was nothing more, Spruce realised, he was going to get from this sane man. He had no fears, apparently, and no vanities. Spruce gazed at him with something like envy. 'If anything further should occur to you...' he ventured.

'I shall of course contact you.' Fresh smiled up at him. Two minutes later Mules edged the Ford gingerly over the ruts toward the main road. We're no forrader,' he said. 'Gold could have doubled back. Riddable could have slipped out again. We've only Fresh's word for it that he came home when he said he did. That woman's very keen on him. She'd certainly lie to protect him.'

Spruce nodded. 'The fact that he didn't have a key, or didn't officially have one, doesn't seem to me to be an impediment to a man like him. He's resourceful. He certainly works in metal, he could have made a copy at some time.'

'What next then?'

'Like I said,' Spruce peered through the rain spattered windscreen, 'the vergers need looking into.'

CHAPTER ELEVEN

DIES IRAE

Theodora gazed into the blank eye sockets of the ram's skull. It stood on Sir Lionel Dunch's table next to a ring of keys. They looked, Theodora thought, like emblems in a seventeenth-century painting.

Sir Lionel leaned across to her and displayed the full horror of his teeth. She thought he was going to pat her knee and so swung her legs out of range. He contented himself with saying with great intimacy, 'I expect you'd like some tea.'

'Lovely,' she murmured with relief.

The room in the manor looked out over formal gardens. Statuary rose out of untrimmed topiary. The gravel paths receding into the distance were weedy. The weather had momentarily cleared. The sun shone. The glass doors on to the terrace were propped open with a bronze statuette of a hussar on camelback about eighteen inches high. It was a beautiful thing in a room full of beautiful things. Cases of coins stretched up one wall. On the other hung a collection of weapons. Theodora could spot Danish, Celtic and mediaeval French work. It was, however, the wall behind the desk which caught her attention. It was covered with bones, animal and human, arranged in patterns of circles and squares. The use of these examples of mortality for decoration struck Theodora as some sort of perversion to which she could put no name.

Sir Lionel busied himself with a silver spirit stove and kettle at the other end of the room. 'I see you admire my memento mori.'

'Unique, surely?'

'Possibly, though there is an account of something rather similar in a Venetian palazzo *circa* 1670 mentioned in Giovanni Sestini's *Antiqua Classica*. We're more squeamish nowadays. I expect there are laws against it. "Health and Safety at Work" like as not. I don't have to bother about that. I have no staff. The collection was started by my grandfather in a more robust age. My father added to it and I have put in the odd femur as they cropped up.'

'You've dug all over the world, Sir Lionel,'

Theodora steered him towards what she hoped would be safer ground. 'I read with great pleasure your *Digging Away*.'

'How kind of you to say so, my dear. Yes, I've dug in a great many places.' Sir Lionel returned to his chair and leaned over the back of it. He eyed Theodora as though she might be a likely site. The kettle began to sing and interrupted whatever more he might have had in mind. He limped off to make the tea.

Theodora wondered how she was going to get what she wanted out of Sir Lionel. She'd hacked out to Quecourt by the afternoon bus to see the bishop suffragan. Bishops made her nervous. She'd known them from her earliest years; suffragan, diocesan, colonial, south Indian, Russian Orthodox and Roman Catholic had all been regularly entertained at her father's house. She must have handed tea and biscuits to scores of them. But she still felt a slight irrational apprehension when she had to deal with them in the line of duty. Nevertheless she had got what she needed in the way of information from Bishop Clement with no difficulty at all. He had shown her the typescript of 'A View from a Pew'. As soon as she saw the typeface, childhood memories had flooded back. It was undoubtedly the product of an ancient Remington. There was just such a machine in the verger's office. It would make perfect sense if one of the vergers had been responsible for the articles. Dennis she discounted on grounds of age, literacy and loyalty. That left Knight or Squires. She did not think she would have much difficulty, armed with the evidence, of finding out which it was. The bishop had said, after some thought, 'I'd like to know, if you find out but unless you feel it relates to poor Vincent's death, it may, as you suggest, be more tactful to let it go. Provided of course it doesn't happen again.' Theodora had been amused at so arbitrary a denial of free speech from so gentle a man.

She had walked the couple of hundred yards across the village green from the bishop's house to Sir Lionel's rather grander establishment wondering whether indeed the articles did have anything to do with Dean Stream's death. She wondered too quite how she was going to account for herself to Sir Lionel. She had no worries about being received. When she had rung at lunchtime to ask if she might see him for a moment, Sir Lionel had been warm in his invitation. But now she was here, how could she put the questions she needed to if her suspicious were to be verified?

'Will you have gleanings from the Janus dig?' she ventured.

Dunch wove his way down the long room, a tarnished silver tray in his arthritic hands. He lowered it carefully to the table before answering.

'I hope, of course, for far more than gleanings. By right the whole thing is mine.'

Theodora raised an eyebrow.

'I mean moral right. My father's activity in the 1922–3 season really made the present find possible. If the dean and chapter had had any sense, they'd have let him dig on then. As it is, I shall expect them to pass the Janus over to me. My collection.' he waved towards the garden, 'is the only possible home for him. He wouldn't feel happy anywhere else. I have just the site for him between two lovely little satyrs beside the low pond at the end of the terrace. He'll be able to see his own reflexion in the water.'

He swung round to Theodora. 'He sings, you know.'

Theodora was startled.

'If you set him up right, when the wind passes through one mouth and out the other, there's a metal stop which acts like a primitive megaphone.'

'Rather eerie.'

'Only to the unsympathetic ear,' Sir Lionel said severely.

'Oh quite.' Theodora felt herself rebuked.

'Are the dean and chapter,' Theodora corrected herself, 'is the chapter going to let you have him, would you say?'

With trembling hand Dunch poured a thin stream of pale gold lapsang into an imari tea bowl and handed it to her. His fingers met hers in the exchange and the contact seemed to enliven him.

'The archdeacon has been in touch. I had quite a hopeful conversation with him actually just before you came. *Entre nous*,' he took the opportunity the phrase afforded him, of leaning closer towards her, 'I think they find him a bit of an embarrassment. The pure pagan power of him,'—he licked his lips—'knocks them out.'

Theodora decided she might as well go to the heart of the matter before the old man had a stroke or worse befell her.

'The other night,' she began, 'the party, the night the dean was killed.'

Dunch was not put off by this change from sex to death. In his seventeenth-century imagination he probably made the closest connexion between the two. His eye kindled.

'Go on, my dear,' he murmured encouragingly.

'Am I right in thinking you stayed on after the party for a while?' She knew very well he'd told Spruce he'd come home with Bishop Clement. She waited.

'Nearly right, my dear,' Sir Lionel closed one complicitous eye. 'I didn't stay on but I did go back. The bronze, you know, it shouldn't be exposed to frost suddenly after fifteen hundred years in the earth.'

Theodora reflected that it had been a lot to hang on an alternative translation of young Riddable's 'archaeologist gentleman' but it seemed to have paid off. She didn't want to appear to be interrogating him, on the other hand she needed times.

She tried, 'Wouldn't it have been rather late?'

'I had a bit of trouble starting the car but she came round in the end,' he smiled at Theodora. 'I suppose I got back to the cathedral about a quarter to one.'

Theodora nodded. Then, to aid the impression of colluding, she risked leaning nearer to him. 'How on earth did you get into the close?'

He was delighted. 'I had my own key.' He gestured towards the ring on the table. 'Had it for years. Well, in fact, it was my father's. They gave him one when he did the initial dig and never reclaimed it.' He guffawed. 'Could have had the altar silver safely stashed away before now.'

'You managed to cover the Janus up safely?'

'Yes, I'd brought a bit of sacking and some tape stuff. He looked a lot more comfortable when I'd finished with him.'

Theodora flung caution to the winds. 'What time would that have been?'

'One-ish. I think I heard it strike.'

'Then you came home?'

'Had a bit of luck as it happened. The lady canon, you know her, thoroughly good sort. Her light was on, so I tapped on her door. Had a noggin to keep the cold out. Then I came home, of course. Can't stay the night with lady canons.'

Theodora sighed. 'That would have been . . .?'

'I left round twoish, I suppose.'

Theodora was incredulous. 'But you must have seen the dean's body by the Janus.'

Sir Lionel was composed. 'No. Why should I? Erica let me out of her front door. Or is it her back door? Well, anyway, she let me out of the door which leads on to Watergate. I didn't go back via the close. Might have caught the murderer if I had, eh.'

'And who would that have been, Sir Lionel?'

'Not popular the new man. No charm of manner.' He smiled across at Theodora in the secure knowledge that he had that quality in large measure.

* * *

'The dean's left instructions in his will for a requiem.' Nick was animated. He was poised to depart, one foot holding open the vestry door, his hands full of choir robes. 'I've never done one.'

Dennis Noble didn't like to admit that he hadn't either. The churchmanship of the last dean but one had not allowed such things. 'We shall need a bit of practice,' he said cautiously. 'The Customary may be a bit out of date.'

'Have you ever done one?'

'Not for a long time. Chapter won't like it. Except for Bishop Clement. He'll know what's right. It'll be a big do, owing to the ...' He trailed off.

'Dramatic ending of the dean.' Nick finished for him. 'Not popular but well known, as you might say.' The cathedral clock struck six. 'Right,' said Nick swinging himself nimbly through the door. 'See you.'

Ten minutes after Nick's departure, Spruce and Mules walked in. Dennis regarded them with distaste. They made him feel guilty. He could not think of what. He'd led a blameless life. He felt it was no proper reward to have found a murdered body in his own close.

Spruce had agreed to let Mules handle the questioning. 'Just a few minutes of your time, Mr Noble,' Mules was murmuring intimately. 'The night of the party.'

'I've told you all I know.'

'You left about seven-thirty, before the guests began to arrive, I think you said.'

'That is correct.' Dennis was verging slowly.

'You weren't needed to serve?'

'The dean only wanted two men. I'd agreed to do the early duty next day. Someone had to. The other two might not have been up to it.'

'You went back to your lodgings at the Aelfric Arms. That's the pub just opposite the Archgate, isn't it?'

'Nice and convenient,' he said defensively. It was a poor do if he had to defend his choice of lodgings.

'Did you hear the dean's guests leaving by any chance?'

'You can hear the archdeacon's XJ out at Quecourt, I should think.'

'And what time would that have been?'

'Twelvish. Little after perhaps.'

'Of course you're very lucky, Mr Noble, living so near you can walk into work. Not many people can do nowadays.' Mules was all sympathetic envy. 'Now how about your colleagues, Mr Squires and Mr Knight. How do they get in?'

'Tristram sometimes walks. Sometimes Nick picks him up on his motor bike. Nick has a motor bike and a push-bike. Depends how early he gets up, I think, as to which he uses.'

'How did they come in on Tuesday night?'

'They didn't. They came in in the morning and stayed on.'

'How did they come in?'

'Nick came in by bike. I think Tristram walked.'

'And how did they go home?'

Dennis stuck. Like a horse forced to a jump he didn't fancy, he would not move forward. Mules approached the problems from the other end.

'What time did they get in on Ash Wednesday, the morning when you found the body?'

Dennis lost his nerve. What with the strain

and the indigestion and the memory of the body which the sergeant's words conjured up, he just wanted to stop these policemen going on and on.

'They didn't stay the night,' he burst out. 'Not Tuesday night.'

Mules looked encouraging.

'It's true they sometimes do. They shouldn't, of course. But it doesn't do anyone any harm. It's a long pull from the bypass, if Nick's doing the early service.'

'You mean they sleep in the cathedral sometimes?'

'Not the cathedral,' Noble was scandalised. 'Here.' He indicated the tiny verger's office. His eye wandered towards the biggest of the cupboards.

'But you don't think Nick did sleep here on Tuesday night.'

'Nick. No.'

'How do you know?'

'I saw him.'

'When?'

'One-ish.'

'What were you doing out at one-ish?'

'I wasn't out. My sitting room is on the top-floor front. I like a pipe before I turn in. Mrs Thrigg doesn't like smoke in the room. I opened the window. I was just going to close it when I saw him.'

'Doing what?'

'He was on his push-bike going like the

clappers down Watergate.'

Mules nodded sympathetically. 'How about Mr Knight? Was he with him?'

'No.'

'And he didn't come past later?'

'Well, he wouldn't need to go to his place. He's the other way up above Colgate.'

'We're very much obliged to you for your help, Mr Noble,' Mules concluded gently. 'And do you happen to know where your colleagues are at the moment?'

Dennis jerked his head upwards in the direction of the cathedral. He felt he'd done enough talking.

As they left, Spruce glanced approvingly at Mules. He was pleased with him. He considered he'd taught him well. There'd been no bullying, just a gentle persistence until the man had come good. They made for the cathedral, one behind the other up the narrow passage. 'In their original statements,' Mules threw back over his shoulder, 'Squires says he left the Deanery at twelve-fifteen and Knight says he went at twelve-thirty.'

'So who's lying? And if it's them, why? They've got about forty minutes to account for.'

Spruce found that he was practically running as they emerged from the passage into the large space of the silent cathedral.

* * *

The lorry in the centre of the close had a hoist on its back. Round it were gathered a knot of knowledgeable helpers. A couple of strong-looking men were padding the hausers where they met the metal of the Janus. Others were busy removing the scaffolding at the base of the plinth on which he rested. The white beams of two building site lamps met and crossed over his head. The light of the early March day was beginning to fade fast.

The young Riddables capered about under the feet of the onlookers half excited by the process of moving him, half sorry to see him go. There was a roar from the hoist and a clanking of chains as they straightened, then the wires tightened and began to take the weight of the bronze.

Mrs Perfect, leaving the office late, put her shopping down and watched as the Janus swung in the air. He spun round slowly first to the north and then to the south as though taking leave of his domain. She'd got used to him. She'd rather liked him. He was a handsome fellow. She could just make out the figure of Oliver Fresh reaching out to guide the frail-looking cradle on to the back of the lorry. Lights from the offices and houses round the close began to flick on. There was a ragged cheer as the cradle bumped gently on to the lorry floor.

The window over the Archgate flew open

and a voice which was not used to being ignored shouted, 'What are you doing? You men, there?'

Theodora who had just stepped through the Archgate and still had half her mind on her meeting with Sir Lionel did not immediately grasp what was happening. She looked up at the open window directly above her. The formidable outline of Canon Millhaven could be made out in the gathering gloom as it leant out towards the lorry and its load in the centre of the close.

The lorry revved its engine. The two large men slapped the tailgates up and ran the bolts home. The little crowd stood back.

'Goodbye. Goodbye, Janus,' shouted the young Riddables cavorting round the wheels.

The lorry bumped on its way over the green sward, leaving deep ruts in the soft turf. It gathered speed and stability as it reached the gravel path and moved with increasing confidence towards the Archgate. Theodora stood aside to let it pass. In the cabin she caught a glimpse of Kevin from the Hollow. The driver, on the other side, she could not see. As the lorry moved past her, Fresh smiled down and raised his hand in courteous salute. They had scarcely reached the main road when the door at the base of the Archgate flew open and Canon Millhaven burst out.

'Stop that lorry,' she called to Theodora, who felt the canon overestimated her powers.

'They have no vestige of a right to remove the Janus. It is the chapter's decision and chapter has not yet met, never mind decided.'

Canon Millhaven's many different pieces of clothing swirled round her mirroring her agitation. She seized Theodora by the elbow. 'Find me a taxi,' she commanded. 'They shall not get away.'

Theodora looked up the street praying that there would be no taxi to be had. An empty taxi edged slowly out of the magistrates' court park and gathered speed as it came towards them. Canon Millhaven raised an imperious and effective arm and tumbled Theodora into the passenger seat. Then she leaned forward and said to the driver, 'Follow that lorry.' The driver turned a blank face towards her. Theodora caught the glint of light on deaf aid and recognised him from her arrival at Bow three days ago.

'He's deaf,' she said to Canon Millhaven, hoping they could all now go home for tea.

'Ah yes, quite so,' said the terrible woman and signed rapidly and explicitly her intentions. The driver smiled broadly and let in the clutch. They shot down Watergate.

Spruce and Mules, emerging on to the steps of the cathedral, were in time to see the lorry bump off the turf. Spruce looked up at the driver's cabin as it passed within ten yards of him. The light was almost gone now but he recognised the face of the driver though not that of his mate. 'He's there,' he said to Mules indicating the rapidly disappearing head of Tristram. 'Get a car and let's get after him.'

Nick, descending the steps of the cathedral a few moments later, was just in time to bump into Mrs Riddable as she streaked across the disfigured turf from the Precentory towards the Archgate.

'They've taken Timothy,' she panted, her thin hair floating out behind her. 'Stop, them, oh, stop them. She turned to Nick who, whilst finding the theatricality a bit difficult to cope with, was rather flattered at her trust in him.

'Who? Where?' he temporised.

'Those *gypsies*,' she italicised. 'Heaven *knows* where they are taking him. In the lorry,' she concluded.

Nick considered his options. 'I've only got a motor bike,' he said tentatively. 'Can you ride pillion?'

'I can do anything for my children!' Mrs Riddable entered her role with zest.

It was fully five minutes after the departure of the lorry that Nick and Mrs Riddable, her arms locked vice-like round his waist, set off on his ancient BMW motor bike down Watergate.

'Which way?' he asked with as much breath as her grip would allow him to draw. She stabbed with her head into the rush-hour traffic thickening in front of them. 'Just keep going, I'll tell you.'

With some trepidation he turned the throttle

and headed out into the darkness.

* * *

Inspector Spruce, had he but known it, was travelling in comparative luxury. He had his own car with the competent Mules at the wheel.

'Where is it going?' Mules asked.

It was a question echoed by each of the other pursuers. Theodora, reflecting on her conversation with Sir Lionel, responded to Canon Millhaven's inquiry that she thought it might be bound for Quecourt. Spruce, conjuring up a memory of lorries with cranes on them lined up beside the entrance to the Hollow, reckoned it might be going back to the Hollow. Young Timothy Riddable, holding Oliver Fresh's hand as they bumped along in the back with the Janus towering above them, didn't much mind where he was going, he was so happy.

In the end it was the earth works which did for the pursuers. A succession of temporary traffic lights and articulateds manoeuvring through inadequately marked coned lanes parted each of them from their quarry.

'We shall press on in faith,' said Canon Millhaven stalwartly as she signed to the driver to take the Quecourt turning.

'How about using the siren?' Mules suggested in exasperation after the third red light in a row.

'Can't see how it would benefit us,' Spruce answered squinting out at the mounds of paving stones and tarmac stacked on either hand. 'We need a tank really.'

'I can't see terribly much,' Nick flung over his shoulder to his helmeted passenger.

'That man Fresh lives at the Hollow. That's where they'll have abducted my boy to. Turn left at the next lights,' Mrs Riddable returned.

* * *

The lurcher bitch roused herself from her slumbers and gave her contralto bark as she heard the lorry grinding up the path. A fair amount of male shouting stimulated yet more barking. Stella put down her pastry knife and flung open the door. The lorry was reversing cautiously round the side of the hut. The Janus in its rickety cradle was swaying to and fro as though on a rough sea.

Fresh waved a cheery hand. 'Safe and sound,' he said. 'Not long now.'

'Are you going to unload him before you eat?'

'Yes. Fifteen minutes. Put all the lights on inside, can you, we're a bit in the dark out here.'

'How many for supper?' she inquired peering into the darkness.

'Three besides us at the moment. There may

be one or two more later. Hello, sweetie.' He greeted the bitch weaving in and out of his legs. 'Now don't get under our feet, there's a good girl. Our new god must weigh about a quarter of a ton.'

It was clear to Stella that Oliver was absolutely delighted to be entertaining the Janus. Indeed she too felt a lifting of the spirit. It was exciting. She turned the oven down and went out to watch operations.

The lorry had halted as close to the back door of the hut as possible. The plan was to swing the Janus through the door into Fresh's workshop. A grinding noise signalled Kevin's attempts to put the hoist into gear. Tristram jumped down from the cabin and unbolted the tail gate. It was nicely judged. There was no gap between the tail board and the threshold of the door. Oliver tapped on the back window of the cabin to alert Kevin. Then he and Timothy watched as the hoist rose and the hausers tightened. Slowly the Janus in his cradle began to rise in the air. Timothy hopped on to the side of the lorry and sat astride it to get a better view as it came down towards the tail gate. At one and the same moment he overbalanced and there was a rending sound of timber splitting. There was an almighty crash and the sound of a car pulling up and a police siren beginning to whine.

Stella stumbled round the far side of the lorry. The Janus lay on its side, the profile of both its faces clearly etched in the light from the house. Timothy was crouched beside it crying. Under it, pinned by head and shoulder could be seen the undoubtedly dead figure of Tristram Knight.

CHAPTER TWELVE

THE QUICK AND THE DEAD

'I haven't made an arrest,' Spruce said.

Theodora poured him a generous single malt and threw a log on the fire in her clerical flat. It was late. The cathedral clock had struck eleven. They were both tired.

'It could have been Riddable,' Theodora was putting it to him. Decks were being cleared.

'Because?'

'I had another message from Ivan Markewicz, this lunchtime. He's a mine of useful information. He tells me he discovered Riddable had applied for a post as principal of a theological college in the north of England. To be sure of an interview let alone an appointment, it had been indicated to him that he would have to have published rather more substantially than he has.'

'So he needed another article in some journal?'

'Right. So when the dean said it was no good it would have stymied Riddable's ambitions.'

'So Riddable's interview with the dean might have been to persuade him to alter his view?'

'Markewicz needed to know the dean's final view before the tenth of March.'

'And he was killed on the ninth,' Spruce said. 'But surely that wouldn't help Riddable much. What he needed was a dean writing in his favour not a dean dead. And there must be other authorities on church history apart from the dean.'

'I quite agree. Unless you posit that Riddable was so angry that he didn't know what he was doing, I don't think it's terribly likely that he killed him. For example, he would have had to keep his anger going long enough to return to his house, find a weapon and go back for another meeting with the dean outside the cathedral.'

'My experience of Riddable,' said Spruce thoughtfully, 'is that if you leave time for the adrenalin to subside, he's not going to go to extremes.'

'Quite so. So what do you make of the other two probabilities, Archdeacon Gold and Oliver Fresh?'

'Gold may be a rather muddled little book keeper,—our accountant chap agrees with you—but I don't see him as a murderer. Quite apart from the tightness of the timing.'

Theodora nodded. 'And Fresh?'

'Capable of anything. But . . .' Spruce paused to formulate his reservations. 'I mean I can see him fighting the dean in the columns of the press. I can see him picketing the cathedral or driving goats through the close or some such, but would he really think that the Hollow would be safe or the cathedral left alone if the dean were dead? He strikes me in many ways as a very rational man.'

'I think then, we're agreed, Inspector.' Theodora looked at him over her glass. Then she said slowly, 'There are too many razors in the vergers' cupboard.'

Spruce nodded. 'I've sent them both for analysis,' he said equably.

'Do I take it Nick and Tristram are in the habit of spending the night there?' Theodora inquired.

'Dennis knew about it and admitted it. When did you notice the razors?'

'The first time I went into the vergers' office. Quite apart from the fact that they cook their morning bacon sandwiches there, there's a cupboard full of sleeping bags. And on the back of the cupboard door there's a shelf with a lot of clutter including those two old-fashioned cutthroat razors as well as one modern one.'

'Were both the cutthroat ones his?'

'No, I think you'll find one was the dean's.'

'What?' Spruce was genuinely surprised.

'If you look on the shelf in the dean's bedroom, you'll find there are no razors at all.'

'A cool fellow and no mistake. So on the night of the murder after they'd both served at the party, he must have gone to the dean's bedroom and taken his razor. Then he waited for him to go to the cathedral, followed him and killed him.'

Theodora shook her head. 'It's more complicated than that.' She put more wood on the fire. Then she reached for a parcel on the table. 'I'm afraid the only tape machine I could find is rather old. It's Canon Millhaven's and must now be of considerable value for its antiquity. However, I think it'll serve.'

Theodora took the reel of tape from the parcel, slotted it into the machine and pressed the appropriate buttons. There was music, a bit of the end of the dean's installation sermon and then a longish pause. Finally came the sound of two people quarreling. The voices of the dean and Canon Millhaven could be heard quite clearly. The dean was saying ... 'refuse to be dictated to in the matter of ordering the cathedral by any weird spiritualistic nonsense.'

'There is nothing weird about your distinguished predecessors,' Canon Millhaven cut in. 'To my mind a dead dean has far more authority than a living one. The words of the dead are tinged with fire.' The dean's voice became more impatient as he replied. 'If you try and stop my proposals being accepted by chapter, I shall have no alternative but to remove you from office.' The next few words were lost then, '... madness ...' could be heard and the tape whirred loose from its reel.

'But I thought ...' Spruce began uneasily. 'I mean, you're not telling me now that Canon Millhaven killed the dean? I thought the razors ... I thought you agreed with me, it's got to be Tristram.'

'Yes, I do agree with you. It was, in my opinion, Tristram. And you may be lucky and find traces of blood on one of the razors. But if you don't, on the evidence you've got you'll have all on to prove it. Whereas I think I have one or two bits of evidence which will help your case.'

'Where did you get that tape? What exactly is it?' Spruce leaned forward. The end was in view.

'It was sent to me anonymously,' Theodora answered, 'care of the cathedral office. It was delivered by hand over the lunch hour today. No one saw the messenger. I picked it up when I got back from my travels to the suffragan and Sir Lionel Dunch this afternoon. I didn't have time to open it until after ...' she paused, 'after the events at the Hollow.'

'So who's it from, do you guess?'

'Oh, I think no doubt about it. It's Nick's all right. He's in charge of the sound system in the cathedral. The basis of the sound system as I understand it is that it's there to amplify preachers. But of course clergy are only human, they like to know what they sounded like when they preached so the custom of recording their utterance from the pulpit has grown up. Naturally the dean wanted to know what his inaugural sounded like, so he ordered a tape. My guess is that the pause button had slipped on the machine and so Nick got more recorded than he bargained for. In particular he seems to have got a dialogue between the dean and Canon Millhaven, probably on the night of the murder.'

'It could have been any time.' Spruce was cautious.

'We'll have to talk to Nick about when he slotted in this particular tape of course. But I'm going on the Riddable boy's evidence that a woman followed the dean out of the cathedral round about one when he was returning to the Deanery. It could have been Millhaven.'

'Why send it to you?'

'That is tricky. At first I thought it might be conscience. If you suspect that the person you love is a murderer and you don't want to move on your own account, might you not send the evidence to an impartial third party?'

'Nick and Tristram were close?' Spruce sounded regretful.

'I think very. However, on reflexion, I wonder if Nick thinks that Tristram was innocent and that this is proof that Canon Millhaven did the killing.'

‘So what’s the proof that she didn’t?’

Theodora considered for a moment. From somewhere below them there came the sound of a door closing. Theodora waited and a moment later there was a hesitant knock. Nick sidled in.

Theodora felt a rush of sympathy which obliterated her anger. ‘Sit down, Nick.’ She poured a rather smaller measure than she had offered to Spruce and added a lot of water. She wanted him relaxed but coherent.

‘I went to the hospital. He was dead when they got him there.’

Both Theodora and Spruce had known that. It had taken all Fresh’s skill to exhume Tristram from beneath the metal of the fallen Janus. Theodora had arrived with Canon Millhaven just as they were finishing the operation. Nick and Mrs Riddable had arrived after the ambulance had taken the body away. Theodora was glad of that. She hoped that they hadn’t let Nick see the body at the hospital. Mrs Riddable had swept Timothy up in her arms and taken him home in a police car. Canon Millhaven had stopped to support Stella. Theodora had taken her deaf taximan back to the Cathedral.

Nick looked round at them bleakly, his face was drained of colour and tight with misery.

‘Would it help to tell us exactly what happened on Tuesday night?’ Theodora noticed how gentle Spruce’s tone was.

‘What would you like to know?’

‘Start with after the guests left.’

‘They’d all gone by twelve. I locked the Archgate then we, Tristram and I, went down to the basement to tidy up and stack the dishes. About ten past twelve, Tristram heard the front door open. He made some remark about guests who forget their umbrellas but I knew it must be someone from the close because I’d locked the gate.’

‘Did the caller ring the bell or knock?’

‘No. I heard the study door open and the sound of voices. I was fairly interested so I mooched upstairs in search of stray glasses. The door of the study wasn’t quite closed. Riddable and the dean were having a splendid set to.’ Nick’s face kindled with pleasure as he remembered. ‘Riddable has quite a good line in offensive oafishness when he wants, but he was no match for the dean’s much more polished performance. “I do not care to imagine what your excellent father would have thought of such carelessness in gathering material and incoherence in its presentation. The avidity with which you rush to display your ignorance of primary sources is distressing; your fractured syntax an embarrassment” type stuff.’ Nick was clearly going to use the insults himself in due course.

‘What was he talking about, did you gather?’

‘Riddable had sent an offering to *Church History Review* and I gather it wasn’t much good in the dean's opinion.'

'Then what?'

Nick's fluency deserted him. Finally he said, 'Well, if you must know we, Tris and I, adjourned to the cathedral, to the vergers' quarters.'

'To spend the night?' Spruce wanted to be clear. 'Was that usual?'

'We only did it sometimes.'

Theodora noticed how Nick turned from being an adult when he was narrating back to a schoolboy when he was answering questions. She had read somewhere that asking a question is a hostile act. Nick certainly seemed to think so.

Nick turned his half-empty glass in his hand and went on. 'We'd just got settled down nicely, when the door handle rattled. It was a nasty moment.' Nick was half defiant half humorous. He clearly hadn't decided, Theodora thought, what his own attitude to his conduct was. 'There was this awful pause when neither of us drew breath. Then footsteps receded up the pasageway. Tris told me to get out. He said he was sure it was the dean and he'd be back with a key. I didn't at all fancy tangling with the dean.'

'So you left?'

'Yes. I absolutely pelted across the close, out of the Archgate and took my bike from the park in the magistrates' court park.'

'What time?'

'I think I heard one strike as I went down Watergate.'

'Your father said...'

'I know, I know. Dad's not too well. He takes sleeping pills. I told him what time I got back. He'd see no reason not to believe me.' Nick had the grace to blush as he met Theodora's eye.

'Have you any idea what happened next? What did Tristram do, for example?'

'He told me what happened, of course. He cleared the room, the vergers' office and took to the main body of the cathedral. The idea was to keep moving around and avoid the dean until he got tired and went to his bed.'

'Hide and seek in the cathedral?'

'Something like that. Tristram told me afterwards. He reckoned the last place the dean would look for him would be his own kitchen. So he went back to the Deanery. He crashed out in the kitchen. It's quite warm. He didn't wake till there was all the hoo ha when his body was found next morning. Well, you know what happened next.' Nick looked across at Theodora.

'What about the tape?' Theo asked.

'What about it?'

'Why did you send it to me?'

'I thought things ought to be cleared up.'

'What do you think it proves, Nick?' Theodora's tone was very gentle.

'It's clear,' Nick's tone was shrill. 'It's

absolutely clear, isn't it? Here,' he reached into the holdall lying beside his chair. 'Look,' he said, 'this is the dean's day-book. Tristram took it on Tuesday night. It's full of references to Millhaven. He wanted her out. He thought she was dotty. There's ample evidence. The tape shows what happened. The dean found Millhaven communing with her dead friends. He started in on her and she flipped her top and knifed him.'

Neither Spruce nor Theodora said a word. Nick looked from one to the other.

Finally Theodora said, 'The dean was killed at ten past one. The watch on his wrist stopped at that time. At one o'clock Canon Millhaven was drinking whisky in her room with Sir Lionel Dunch.'

CHAPTER THIRTEEN

RESURREXIT

'Hallelujah,' shouted the boy sopranos.

'Hallelujah, hallelujah,' returned the lay tenors across the aisle.

Resurrection morning light streamed through the clerestory windows. The heavy scent of lilies filled the building. The procession ambled up the nave at an Anglican pace. Nick was verging for the last time. Tomorrow with any luck he'd be in France heading south. He passed close to Theodora who had managed by Canon Millhaven's good offices to secure a seat at the back of the choir for this Easter Sunday Mattins. Nick did not smile at Theodora but he raised an eyebrow in her direction which she took to be kindly meant. Canon Millhaven herself was processing as the most junior of the residentiary canons.

There were some gaps, of course. They had lost a dean, the archdeacon was not part of the procession. But the diocesan bishop had returned from America and would in due course be preaching. The ministry of the word, Theodora reflected, was so very important but not perhaps quite as important as our actions, which speak louder.

From where she sat she could see the Riddable children with their mother. The children all had a well-scrubbed look. Rebecca was practising being demure, Ben looked as though butter would not melt in his mouth. Timothy, she knew, was to join the choir school next term. He'd told her he was looking forward to that because it meant being in the boarding house and not living at home. Theodora saw his point. Glancing down into the nave she spotted Sir Lionel Dunch, his eyes on the splendid seventeenth-century memorial to L. Dunch Esq, Lord Mayor of the City of Bow in 1694. Well, he'd got his Janus, after all, the fractured remains of it at least, for his collection. Behind him she could see Spruce sitting next to Mules. Spruce looked alert and interested observing the ritual of another tribe.

They sang, they listened, they prayed the splendid words of the collect for Easter Day. The bishop was verged from his throne to the pulpit. The congregation settled itself to follow either the bishop's thoughts or their own.

'"From dust I rise, and out of nothing now awake",' the bishop quoted. 'We have been much beset by death of late. And as you know there are many sorts of death beyond the merely physical. The death of innocence, the death of reputation. And without religion, without the truths of the Christian religion, these sorts of death are insurmountable. Without the Christian hope, we would be condemned to end as bones in the earth.'

Theodora thought of the ram's head and bones hideously decorating Sir Lionel's study. She thought also of the death of the late dean's reputation. A mistake from his past had risen up and brought about his death. While at the same time a Roman god had risen from the abyss and challenged the religion of the clergy showing how very lacking in vitality that religion was.

'What is it,' she returned to hear the bishop ask, 'which can make bones live, which can rescue reputation and recapture innocence? Of this much at least we may be sure, it is nothing that idols can do for us. Our idols, those false and unworthy ideals which we set up for ourselves, power, money, self-importance, those cannot save us eternally. They cannot bring life out of death. Indeed, they are the very instruments of death.'

Theodora thought of the end of Nick's painful recital of the final events of Shrove Tuesday, five weeks ago. Nick had known, she felt sure, in his heart that Tristram had killed the dean. He'd known because he knew of Tristram's past history. St Crispin's refuge had housed Tristram's friend. He'd been one of the men diagnosed with AIDS. He'd died soon after the refuge had been closed. Tristram hadn't gone into the details but Nick had said Tristram's narrative had sounded like an indictment. As far as Tristram had been concerned the dean's action in shutting the house and turning out its inmates was tantamount to killing them. He quite deliberately followed the dean's career and intended revenge. It had seemed to Tristram like Providence itself when Vincent Stream had been appointed to the very cathedral where he would be delivered into his hands.

'Surely what alone gives life, what restores and refreshes', the bishop was pressing on, 'is generosity, generosity and forgiveness. That is what our Lord himself taught us by his words and demonstrated in his life and in his death.'

But however you read the gospel, Theodora reflected, with whatever presuppositions you approach it, there's no doubt but that Jesus was very hard indeed on the traditional leaders of religion and very gentle indeed to those on the fringes of society. Perhaps the institutional forms of religion, the worldly, power-based systems of the church were doomed always to be hostile to the practice of ordinary virtue. When Theodora had challenged Nick with having written the *Bow Examiner* articles he'd said that surely free, critical and truthful debate is the basis of all virtue and the Church is so obsessed with its own importance and rightness that it can't listen. 'I love it dearly,' Nick had said, 'but it won't last my time out if they don't reform.'

'The Church is not a democratic debating society,' Theodora had snapped at him. But she wondered whether he hadn't a point.

'If then we wish to turn from death,' the bishop was saying, 'if we intend to shake ourselves free from enslavement to idols and rise to the life eternal, we must learn to practise humility. Humility comes from a word meaning earth. Earthiness is what we need, a down-to-earth and clear-sighted honesty which prompts us to look both ways, both within ourselves and outwards to our neighbours and our society. Such humility, if constantly worked for in a disciplined life of prayer, is the true mark of the follower of Christ.'

Down beyond Spruce Theodora glimpsed

familiar faces. Surely it was Oliver Fresh and Stella Parish. The chapter, she had learned from the *Examiner*, had got its planning permission for the development of the Hollow as office blocks. If the chapter chose to proceed with their plans the Hollowmen and their animals would soon be homeless. They'd have to move on. Theodora felt a sudden shame. We have the rhetoric, she thought, blaming herself as well as the Church, we've had the words for centuries. It's the actions we're not so good at.

We hope you have enjoyed this Large Print book. Other Chivers Press or Thorndike Press Large Print books are available at your library or directly from the publishers. For more information about current and forthcoming titles, please call or write, without obligation, to:

Chivers Press Limited
Windsor Bridge Road
Bath BA2 3AX
England
Tel. (01225) 335336

OR
Thorndike Press
P.O. Box 159
Thorndike, ME 04986
USA
Tel. (800) 223-6121
(207) 948-2962
(in Maine and Canada, call collect)

All our Large Print titles are designed for easy reading, and all our books are made to last.